# EXCERPTS FROM LETTERS TO THE AUTHOR:

"The constant struggle or fight to try not to smoke anymore is completely gone, and instead I just have no desire to smoke. It's been over 6 months since I quit and I still haven't had an urge to smoke and I don't expect to. What this book did for me was amazing. Nothing short of a miracle."

— Kevin G.

"After smoking two packs a day for over twenty years, I am once again a nonsmoker!!! I still can't believe it. It really works. Thank you, thank you, THANK YOU!"

— Amy M.

"You changed my outlook and thinking on life. To me this is PRICELESS! I'm re-motivated again and it feels wonderful to which I'd like to say thank you very much. It's amazing how this has opened up a new chapter in my life and given me positive energy and thinking. Thank you again."

— Pam T.

"I was not ready to quit smoking, but a friend of mine gave me your book and asked me to read it. I was shocked and surprised how before I even finished reading it I suddenly had absolutely no desire to have another cigarette. I still can't believe how EASY it was."

— Jason H.

"I've read countless books on how to quit smoking, but none comes close to this one in showing you exactly how to do it without feeling deprived or miserable. What is strange is you actually feel better not worse, and you even feel stronger and more in control of everything else in your life."

- Steven D.

"I do not fully know or understand what sparks a caterpillar to evolve into a butterfly, but I do know that in my case, you have played a pivotal role in helping me shed layers of my old skin. Therefore, I know that which you asked me to let go of, was only done so that I can make room for something *more valuable*."

- Jonathan C.

"I really enjoyed reading your book for one very special reason... You spoke from your heart and made it meaningful, impactful, relatable, and REAL!"

- Hovi S.

"This book changed my life. In the past every time I tried to quit smoking I was left feeling angry and depressed, but not this time. This time it was the exact opposite. After going through the steps in the book I started to feel better not worse. This unique method of quitting smoking was so much fun, it actually made me forget I was doing something "healthy". Whoever said "no pain, no gain" obviously has not read this book!"

- Mike B.

"I want to start by saying thank you. Your book allowed me to see other changes I should take to better myself. I enjoyed reading your book... it also gave me the opportunity to re-evaluate certain thoughts, behaviors, and attitudes I hold that could use a change. The book made that happen."

- Guadalupe B.

"Not only is this book helpful to smokers, but to anyone trying to over-come any addiction or difficult stage in their life. I was impressed by the *motivational* aspect of the chapters as well as the creative and inspiring titles. My interest was piqued by the delay in describing "The Secret" and it created the temptation to continue to read more. Your personal stories and struggles are especially *inspirational* and provide a *powerful instrument for change* and a higher degree of authenticity.

I especially enjoyed the easy style of writing. My only regret is that I did not have this information...many years ago!"

- Sheila S.

"*The Secret to Stop Smoking* literally changed my life. I have read a lot of literature in the past about quitting smoking, but never have *I had such a breakthrough and eye opening experience*. The great thing about this book is it goes beyond just smoking, it allows you to carefully look at other elements in your life. It truly helped me in amazing and innumerable ways. I highly recommend this book. It's a must read!"

- Candelaria M.

"A *remarkable* and *inspiring* technique for stopping smoking. As a sincere friend and guide in the book, Dr. Rosiere encourages the reader on a journey through a simple step-by-step technique that will surely help those individuals motivated to quit smoking.

Dr. Rosiere is to be commended for his effort and sincerity in guiding and helping others."

- Dr. Scott Simon Fehr
101 Interventions In Group Therapy
Introduction To Group Therapy: A Practical Guide (2nd Edition)

ISBN: 1439276528
ISBN-13: 9781439276525

# THE SECRET
## To
# STOP SMOKING

## UNLEASH YOUR POWER

How To Take Immediate Control of Your Smoking
Without Stress, Cravings, or Weight Gain

By Dr. Scott C. Rosiere

"All truths are easy to understand once they are discovered;
the point is to discover them."
- Galileo Galilei, *Italian astronomer & physicist (1564 – 1642)*


"You shall know the truth, and the truth will set you free."
- Ancient Scripture

# DEDICATION

This book is dedicated to everyone who currently smokes and has even the smallest desire to quit.

And to my wife Mona, who first inspired me to find the way to put *The Secret to Stop Smoking* into words that ultimately leads the way to freedom.

# CONTENTS

## PART THREE

# Acknowledgements

This book was from the very start a labor of love. Fortunately, I did not have to go it alone. From the outset I was blessed with help and guidance from a creative source, or *guiding spirit*, that assisted me in the process of writing this book. I believe it could not have been possible otherwise. For this, I am most grateful.

I have also been blessed to have the help of many fine people. They are the original source of many of the insights embedded within the message of this book.

First, I wish to thank my children, India and Hunter. Their untamed spirit and intense passion toward life allowed me to see more clearly through their eyes what I was not always able to see through my own.

I would like to express my love and admiration to my wife Mona, for her unwavering love and support of me through the good times, as well as the challenging times.

To my parents, who have always been there for me, and taught me valuable life lessons in the most powerful way possible, by example. They have shown me what is truly most valuable in this world can neither be bought or sold, but only freely given away to those you love.

I would also like to express my deep appreciation to my mentor, Dr. Scott Simon Fehr. His wisdom, genuineness, and compassion are unparalleled.

I offer special thanks to my trusted friend and collaborator, Nico Gertie. I am extremely grateful for your companionship and many insightful recommendations during those long hours of research. I believe this book is exponentially improved because of your generous investment.

I am especially grateful to my first-class editor, Sue Mosebar. Sue is a master wordsmith at the height of her profession. She possesses a genuine passion for the written word and an astonishing ability to transform my mangled manuscript into the clear, compelling and creative text you see throughout this book.

Also, I would like to offer my sincere debt of gratitude to all my students, clients, and colleagues who have been incredibly generous and supportive in helping to make this endeavor possible. I appreciate all your warmth, kindness and compassion. You have helped me to gain a better understanding of the nature of the most addictive and deadly drug on our planet, and in the process further shed light on how to help others escape its deadly grip. Many people will greatly benefit due to your compassion; of this I am certain.

# PREFACE

*"I really need to stop smoking."*

Have you ever attempted to stop smoking before?

How may times after continuing to smoke afterwards did you say to yourself, "I can quit if I really want to, I'm just not ready to stop smoking right now."

If this scenario sounds even remotely familiar, know this: you are not alone.

Ask people why they continue to smoke, and the majority of smokers will tell you they "enjoy" smoking, and they may further explain that they simply "choose" to smoke. Perhaps if they looked just a little deeper below the surface, they would find that in reality they are no longer in control. Instead, it is very much the other way around.

Now, what if I provided you with a proven method to overcome the obstacles smokers face and armed you with a flawless plan that has helped transform the lives of thousands of people and instantaneously and permanently returned them back to their natural-born state of being nonsmokers again?

What if I showed you precisely how to regain control over your smoking and secure complete control over your life?

And, what if I could show you exactly how to do this without having to suffer nicotine cravings, weight gain, or additional stress? You see, there really is no need to turn your world upside-down once you discover the secret to stop smoking.

Moreover, you have absolutely nothing to lose: you don't even have to slow down or stop smoking while you are reading this book. If, at the end, you decide to continue to smoke, you'll be none the worse off.

Think about it... what do you have to lose by just learning about this remarkable and revolutionary system that has been recommended by doctors and pharmacists from around the world?

Imagine waking up in the morning and feeling stronger, more energetic, and confident than ever before. Imagine after going through this process having a newfound source of energy to do all of the things you have been putting off accomplishing in your life. Imagine having the power and ability to take immediate action on anything you desire and set your mind to, and know you will come out on top.

Know this, you absolutely can have all of this, and more. Without question, you have the ability to change your life in every respect. It doesn't matter if you have been smoking for two years or forty-two years. What does matter is that you have the desire to feel and look healthier, to lower your risk for lung and heart disease, and to restore your mind and body.

Without question, you do have the capacity to take back control over your life.

Learn from the thousands of men and women who have used the techniques described in these pages. In doing so, they have radically transformed their lives for the better. By implementing the simple steps and universal principles detailed throughout the book, they have mastered the skills necessary to be successful. Their accomplishments are proof that once you learn the secret to stop smoking, you too will have the power to succeed.

Now that you realize what is possible, are you ready to let me help you discover your true potential?

If so, I promise to show you every shortcut and explain exactly how to avoid all the traps, so you are in a position to ultimately achieve your goal.

When you decide to take this step, you are giving yourself the ultimate gift–the capacity to live a happier, healthier, and more prosperous life. You will begin unleashing your true power and restoring your body and mind back to your natural-born state: that of a nonsmoker.

The process of taking back total control over your smoking and your entire life begins the moment you turn this page...

# INTRODUCTION

Imagine one night in the not so distant future, after learning of a powerful, little known secret... You fall asleep, and soon, an amazing transformation occurs within you.

A transformation so remarkable it positively impacts the quality of the rest of your life.

As you awake the next morning, much to your surprise, almost as if a miracle had occurred, you no longer have the urge to smoke... *ever again*!

Rest assured, this is not some unattainable dream or fantasy. In fact, it happened to me precisely this way, and it had an instant and profound impact on *every aspect of my life* thereafter. Now, I often think of how fortunate I was to have personally experienced it because of all the ways I have since benefited from its power.

There may be a part of you that finds this hard to believe. I understand. But as you continue to read this book, you will begin to quickly see just how this was possible, and how easily you can enjoy the same experience.

Once you learn this secret, you'll have the ability to instantaneously return to your natural state of being. You'll be a nonsmoker once again. Better yet, it will also *change the entire course of your future* by helping you experience dramatically improved health, energy, wealth, vitality, passion, and so much more.

You see, the very act of picking up this book suggests that somewhere inside you is a burning desire for something more in your life. Deep inside, a desire to make a significant change for the better. It is my hope you will permit me to help you turn this budding aspiration into an absolute reality.

What if I could provide you with a specific set of simple steps and a decisive plan proven time and time again to produce startling results for thousands of people from all over the world?

Would you be interested in hearing more about it?

I know this change can happen because I have been able to do so in my own life, and I have also had the opportunity to help thousands of people just like you.

## The Opportunity of a Lifetime

Just in case these claims sound too good to be true, let me quickly share a story about a person who once found himself face to face with an opportunity like this–the opportunity of a lifetime. Yet if not for his willingness to suspend judgment and follow his curiosity, he could have easily let one of the greatest gifts pass him by.

On a cold January morning in 1905, Captain Fredrick Wells, Superintendent of the Premier Diamond Mine near Pretoria, South Africa, was making his daily rounds when, suddenly out of the corner of his eye, a tiny sparkle of light caught his attention.

For a second, he thought maybe he had just imagined the light. Deciding he would make another attempt to find it, he turned around and held his lantern high above his head, and suddenly, he again saw the most magnificent sparkle.

Upon closer inspection, Captain Wells thought it was probably just a chunk of broken glass or something of equally little value. He wondered to himself if the other mine workers were playing a practical joke on him.

Though almost certain it was not real, he pried the object out of the wall with his pocketknife and sent the rather large piece of glass to be analyzed. It was later determined the glass was actually a perfectly clear and colorless *diamond*. Weighing an astonishing 3,106 carats, it was confirmed to be the largest diamond known to exist in the world.

The Cullinan Diamond, as it was later named, remains the biggest and most precious diamond ever discovered. The largest and most remarkable gem in the world was found by what some would attribute to as a "chance" opportunity.

You see, Captain Wells just as easily could have walked right by the largest and most valuable diamond in the world had he not allowed himself to suspend his own doubt and disbelief.

## Stacking the Deck in Your Favor

Similarly, there exists a mysterious and little-known secret to stop smoking, which has just as much value, if not more, as the Cullinan Diamond. Few people know it even exists. If only the many people desperately trying to quit smoking were to discover it and learn its true value, they could in a very short period of time completely remove their desire to smoke forever.

Even if at this moment you have not yet made the decision to quit smoking, wouldn't knowledge of this fail-proof and simple method be extremely useful when the day comes that you do decide to quit?

Consider for a moment that you really have very little to lose by just taking the short time it takes to learn about this revelation, which has already helped countless people quit smoking for good.

And, if after learning of its power, you still wish to continue smoking, you will be none the worse off. In reality, you will be ahead of the game, and here is why…

Independent scientific research has consistently demonstrated over the past 25 years that less than four out of every 100 smokers who attempt to quit on their own are able to do so for longer than six months in any given year. This statistic holds true for everyone in every country all over the world—regardless of their strength of willpower or commitment to quit smoking.

This statistic is even more remarkable when you consider that two in three smokers report a desire to quit.

Now take a second to reflect on this for a moment… Why do so many smokers fail? Why is there such a disparity between what they say they want to do and what they are able to accomplish?

How is it possible that in this modern era when surgeons have the technology and skill to remove an individual's diseased heart from the body and transplant it with a healthy heart, and scientists can safely land a man on the surface of the moon, there is no modern medical intervention than can *cure* people who truly want to stop smoking?

Of course there are some medical interventions, such as nicotine replacement therapy (nicotine patch, pills, and gum) that can double the chances, but even that is only around eight out of every 100 who are successful.

I don't know about you, but I wouldn't even attempt to cross my street if I thought there was only an eight percent chance I would make it to the other side of the road.

It's easy to understand why so many smokers are discouraged! Yet now there is a way to dramatically increase your odds of success. You see, there are some clear and recognizable reasons cigarette smokers find it so difficult to quit.

Once you become aware of these reasons, you will begin to understand the initial steps needed to overcome this destructive force. In fact, this intervention is so powerful and effective, it can help almost anyone. The small fraction of people who will likely not be able to benefit from this method are only those individuals who are incapable or unwilling to understand.

## What Worked for Me and Countless Others *Will* Work for You too

Best of all, this powerful method is right at your very fingertips. It is based on a clear and precise understanding of just what all those who have been successful had to do to become nonsmokers again.

If not for my many years of training as a clinical psychologist and my terrible misfortune in a particular business endeavor which threatened to leave my family and me bankrupt and homeless, I too would likely still be searching for a way to stop smoking.

As you read further on and learn what I have uncovered, you will be amazed by the ease at which this very transformation can take place for you. There may be a part of you still wondering whether this could really be true, and I don't blame you.

There are many false promises out there from people selling products that claim they can help you stop smoking but in reality just do not work. Or maybe you have tried to quit smoking many times before on your own only to fall right back into the same vicious cycle of smoking all over again.

Who could blame you for having doubts? Had this transformation not already happened for me, I would have the very same doubts myself. Fortunately, I can say with unwavering confidence, because of my experience and the remarkably powerful insights uncovered during them, everything I share with you in this book actually occurred for me and can just as easily happen for you.

Yet I still encourage you to question everything presented to you from here on in. In fact, it is essential that you start to pay more attention and look more closely at everything you have ever been told by others about smoking, including what you yourself have come to believe about the nature of why you continue to smoke cigarettes.

After having my first cigarette at the age 14 and then turning this occasional habit into a full-blown addiction, I would have been the last one to ever consider this possible. After all the horror stories that have been spread like folk tales of how incredibly hard it is to quit smoking and how painful the withdrawal from nicotine can be, it seemed an absolute impossibility that such a fast and painless method could ever exist. But let me assure you it does. Moreover, it works for every single person who uses it correctly.

*The Secret is not so much a "secret" as it is a precise understanding and application of seven natural laws which govern the process one must go through to leave smoking behind for good—without a lifetime of persistent urges, weight gain, or sporadic relapses.*

This method is scientifically based and was discovered through a deductive reasoning process found by comparing and analyzing the successful methods implemented by myself and the group of individuals mentioned earlier.

The common elements uncovered are shared in this book. They are based entirely on proven universal principles, much like those that underlie the laws of gravity. Just as gravity exerts force on everything on our planet, regardless of whether or not one understands the mechanics of how it works. The same holds true for difficulty or ease the smoker attempting to quit will experience depending on the type of approach used. Just as we know that when we throw an object up in the air, it will always eventually fall back down to the ground, the same consistency holds true for implementing this system: when applied properly, it works *every time*, without exception.

Fortunately, this breakthrough method can be applied by anyone regardless of age, willpower, or how long one has been a smoker. It takes only the desire and commitment to put these steps into action. You don't have to suffer any painful withdraw symptoms or mental anguish–simply follow the steps and experience this naturally occurring phenomenon.

## I Have Been Where You Are Now

Let me take a moment to briefly explain how I came to write this book. After I had first escaped my own addiction to cigarettes, I was elated to be free from this nightmare. Free from the morning coughing fits, free of the head-throbbing pain, free of the bad breath and constant feeling of fatigue and misery. Even more I was free from the growing fear in the back of my mind of the potential irreversible damage I was causing to my body.

But most important of all, I was free from the constant *insatiable urge* to smoke. Finally I had been released from the miserable trap I had been stuck in for so many years.

Back when I was still smoking, I would wake up and drag myself out of bed and feel like a zombie until I had that first cigarette and then eased into the day. And from there I would go on to plan throughout the rest of the day when I would have the next cigarette and the next and the next… until I was literally right back in my bed again.

My chain smoking had become so damaging to my health that I had started having regular bouts of vertigo, which felt as if the entire room was spinning out of control. I sometimes had days where the vertigo was so bad I could not even drive to work for fear of driving off the road, or worse, driving head on into another car.

Soon after quitting, each day began with a renewed excitement and a restoration to health and energy, back to levels I had not had since I was a teenager. Since leaving smoking behind for good, I now spring out of bed with passion looking forward to the day ahead, sometimes getting so much done and having so much fun that I often don't even want to go to sleep because there is so much more I want to still do. And the bouts of vertigo? Gone for good!

Looking around at others still caught in the grips of this nightmare, I began wanting to share this simple and painless way to escape. How could I not try to help? You see, I had family and friends I loved very much who were being held prisoner by the insatiable cravings that always haunt the cigarette smoker.

I began to wonder, wouldn't *everyone* want to know this simple and easy way out?

What I later learned was that a few of the people still stuck in this sinister trap were hesitant to even attempt to stop smoking. For some reason, unknown to me at the time, they were reluctant to try. **It was only much later I came to realize the intense and often paralyzing fear some people possessed because they attributed great pain from their nicotine oppressor if they were even to think about escaping.**

Because of the many years of unsuccessful attempts to quit smoking using all the other ineffective methods, many of these people no longer wanted to get their hopes up of finally kicking this horrible habit... only to then have their hopes shattered yet again.

For some of the long-time smokers who had years ago given up even trying to resist, there was a long-held disbelief that anything could ever work for them. They had lost all hope that they could ever quit.

They felt a sense of having received a life-term of imprisonment without the chance of parole.

One of those people still imprisoned was my wife, the mother of my two children, whom I love very much. She had been a smoker for over twenty years and was still ensnared in this dreadful trap. I could no more leave her behind than you could leave someone you love behind in a burning building, especially knowing a way to safely get them out.

As each day passed and I felt healthier and stronger, it became increasingly difficult to stand back and watch her remain stuck in this dark abyss. This is what prompted my journey to find out what precisely had taken place for me and how I could find a way to make it happen just as easily for her and everyone else looking to be free of this evil tyrant.

I knew if I could just write down the exact steps that had helped me so easily escape, it would be just like an emergency escape route, which could safely lead the way out for everyone.

I was determined to spread the insight to everyone who would listen. To my great surprise, many people joined this cause and helped make this book possible.

You see, there are really only a small handful of people who greatly benefit from your remaining dependent on the nicotine in cigarettes. They are a small few who are not too different from the slave traders of the past. They sell you into a life of bondage for their own profit and financial gain. The tobacco companies, the advertisers, and even to some degree, the ones we entrust to look out for our best interests, like some doctors and government officials who mostly support nicotine replacement treatments and expensive pharmaceutical products that rarely work.

You may or may not know that last year just four tobacco companies alone sold over **100 Billion Dollars** worth of cigarettes! In the U.S., the federal government collected over 8 Billion Dollars in tax revenue from the sale of tobacco, and this does not include the billions of dollars the 50 individual states collected from state taxes on the legal sale of cigarettes.

This has created a built-in conflict of interest. Yet you should know there were many more compassionate and courageous people who have helped me along the way to uncover and spread *The Secret to Stop Smoking* around the world. I am very grateful to all of them for helping make this book a reality.

## Congratulations for Taking This Powerful Step to Improve Your Life

I want to stop and take a moment to tell you how much I admire and respect your desire to quit smoking and your willingness to seek out information that will help you accomplish this. I believe you and I share some similar dreams and goals about how we want to live the rest of our lives. I believe you want to have a happier, healthier, and more enjoyable life.

It is because of how much I value these shared goals that I would be honored if you would allow me to be your guide, or *coach*, at your side as you begin the process of becoming a nonsmoker once again.

It is my sincere hope you will take me up on this offer. If you do, I know you will learn to avoid the many traps that most others fall prey to, at their own peril. You see, I believe it is not really your fault that you have been unable to quit up to this point.

There are numerous obstacles that have been *intentionally* put in your way in an attempt to prevent you from ever quitting. However, with access to the knowledge, insight, and powerful inspiration contained in the following pages, you will soon learn how truly simple it can be to overcome them and succeed.

As you continue to read, you will learn more about *The Secret* that I and countless others have since uncovered which has allowed us the ability to immediately transform our lives.

You will soon realize that this was not just possible for us, but that it is practically guaranteed to happen for you as well. And all you need to do is simply apply what you learn.

It's that easy!

However, there is one thing you must do to learn to use this life-changing force. While this initial step is not that difficult and costs practically nothing, it is, nonetheless, essential for it to be revealed to you.

Fortunately, the only thing you need do is really quite easy. **All you must do is maintain an open mind and follow the simple steps included in this book.**

Nothing more, and nothing less.

So it is with great respect, admiration, and excitement that I extend to you an invitation to acquire these remarkable insights because I know how they can quickly change your life for the better. Come see for yourself just how remarkable the transformation in you will be.

There really is nothing to lose, and so very much to benefit from by embarking on this journey.

Just imagine if Captain Fredrick Wells had pushed aside his curiosity to find the source of sparkling light that had briefly caught his attention on that cold January morning in 1905. He would have missed discovering the most precious diamond in existence, which glinted only a few feet in front of him.

This same type of remarkable discovery lay just in front of you. At this very moment, there waits for you a golden opportunity to unearth a secret so significant its power can provide you with a lifetime of personal benefits beyond what any words could ever describe.

Go ahead and reach for it–you will not be disappointed. In fact, you will be greatly rewarded for the effort. Turn the page to begin...

# Part One

# 1

## THE IRRESISTIBLE OFFER

Life can be stressful! There is no escaping this single fact. From practically the first minute you wake in the morning, you are faced with pressures and demands that at times can seem overwhelming and never ending.

Some of these demands come from simply having to meet our very basic needs for food, shelter, and protection. Others come from our interactions with family, friends, and people we work with. And some demands we unknowingly place on ourselves.

As if this were not bad enough, the news media, politicians, and advertising industry repeatedly remind us of our stresses and shortcomings and even blow them out of true proportion in an attempt to get us to buy their newest products, take their latest pills, and yes, smoke their recently lowered price cigarettes at the local gas station.

You have seen the ads: buy two packs of smokes and get the third pack free. They know we are always looking for a good deal. So while you may have been working up the steam to finally quit smoking once and for all, you find yourself instead driving away with three packs of cigarettes instead of the one pack you were trying not to buy to begin with.

This is no accident, by the way. The cigarette companies spend a staggering 13 billion dollars a year in advertising and promotions to get us to do one thing and one thing only: buy cigarettes, and lots of them. As I said, life is full of challenges and stress.

All right, I could go on and on and on about how stressful life is, but I think you already know this. Everybody is already experiencing stress—some more than others. All stress is relative, and so what seems stressful to you may not seem so to someone else, and vice versa. But trust me, they are stressed out too!

So how does all this talk about stress relate to your figuring out how to finally stop smoking cigarettes?

Maybe you are thinking to yourself right now, "Hey, I smoke to deal with all this stress!" or "If I stop smoking, I'll just be more stressed out." Maybe you're thinking, "I have tried to quit and nothing works!" Or maybe you're even thinking, "Hey buddy, don't you know that quitting smoking is way too hard and only stresses you out even more?"

My response to that last question is, yes, I do know. I remember how so many of my attempts to quit smoking never worked out, and how each failed attempt made me want to give up trying ever again. I also remember all the ridiculous games I would create in my head to try to trick myself into not smoking any more. I vividly recall how none of these attempts ever worked.

Okay, if you haven't just thrown the book down and walked away yet, let me quickly add that while my many previous attempts to quit smoking never worked, the very first time I stumbled across *The Secret to Stop Smoking* and used it, it did work. And I haven't had the urge to smoke since.

Here I would like to add what I consider a built-in bonus of this unique method and make this offer to those readers who have not yet made a firm commitment to quit smoking. The majority of people I interview often give several commonly shared reasons why they continue to smoke. These reasons often fall into the following general categories:

- "I enjoy smoking because it helps me to relax."
- "Smoking helps me concentrate and deal with stress."
- "It helps me wake up in the morning and energizes me throughout the day."
- "I can't imagine not having a cigarette with my morning cup of coffee or after a meal."
- "Smoking helps relieve boredom."

Okay, here is the offer: *What if there were a way to get all these exact same benefits you currently attribute to smoking, and much more, but you could get them without having any of the negative side effects that have been proven to exist with long-term smoking?*

Would you at least be interested in hearing more about how this is possible?

If so, what *The Secret* can make possible for you is to instantly remove any desire you have to continue to smoke without turning your world upside-down. It can do this while also satisfying all your needs previously mentioned for why most people continue to smoke.

You see, when you have a method that is superior, you no longer have a need or desire to use the old one. For instance, some years ago, whenever you were away from your home and you needed to contact someone, you likely used a pay phone to call. Since technology has created the compact and affordable cellular phone, almost everyone carries one everywhere they go. With this more convenient and efficient technology, it is likely you have not had the need nor desire to use a payphone in a long, long time; whereas in the past you may have used a pay phone on a somewhat regular basis.

The same holds true for the tools you will be provided with here as with other advanced technologies. Once you learn *The Secret to Stop Smoking,* you will no longer have the need nor desire to smoke to achieve the state of relaxation, to aid concentration, or as a means of relieving boredom. Even better, when you gain control of your smoking, you will gain control of your LIFE.

My hope is that as more and more people learn *The Secret*, there will no longer be a desire for anyone to ever smoke again. And one day, a later generation will look back at our particular time period and think to themselves, "How peculiar people used to be with all their smoking." It will be as foreign to them as it is to us when we watch an old black and white movie and see someone walk into a phone booth or use a telegraph to send a message.

*The Secret* will one day make smoking obsolete.

This book is about a clinical psychologist's journey into the smoky underground world of stress, cigarettes, and dissatisfaction, and the eventual discovery of a previously little known yet powerful cure to stop smoking. I will take you on this journey and share with you just what I learned there, and what I've learned from the growing number of others who have since made this same discovery and quit smoking for good. As you read on, you will find how you too can start living your life smoke-free.

"No matter who you are, no matter how long you've been a smoker, you absolutely do have the power to become a nonsmoker again."

-Dr. Scott C. Rosiere

# 2

---

# A PURPOSE-DRIVEN LIFE

"If you always do what you've always done, you'll always get what you've always got… Is that what you really want?"

-Anonymous

## Why do most attempts to stop smoking fail?

The answer to this question might surprise you. Unfortunately, like most interventions in modern medicine, the focus on helping individuals quit smoking cigarettes has predominantly been on stopping the symptom rather than removing the underlying cause that created the symptom to begin with.

In other words, we focus all of our attention on just putting out the fire, instead of looking for what started the fire in the first place, so it doesn't start again!

The reason this practice goes on so often is because most of us don't notice a small but growing problem until it's much too late. And by then, we don't really care what initially started the problem, or what's keeping it going… We just want it to stop causing us pain right now! And that makes sense. *Or does it?*

I have seen this unfold in my private practice time and time again. An individual seeks my help to get relief from something that has become extremely painful to him or her. More often than not, it's reached a point where he is experiencing unbearable negative consequences in his life. At first he doesn't really want to focus any of his time, energy, or effort on understanding or eliminating the underlying source of the behaviors that first brought on these negative reactions. Furthermore, he doesn't really understand why he even started engaging in these original behaviors in the first place, which now he is reluctant to change.

Okay, here we could get lost in dissecting the psychological roots of all behavior, but that would take us too far away from our current mission, which is to stop smoking now. So let's look quickly at two very important concepts we will need to better understand to accomplish our goal. Because once you learn these two insights, you will be on your way toward success.

## Purpose-Driven Behavior

First, among most psychologists, there is a basic understanding that *all behavior is purpose driven*. This awareness that every single behavior we engage in throughout the day is intentional, or rather has a specific purpose, is an essential insight needed to begin to unlock the secret to quitting for good. Not one single behavior we engage in is accidental or random. There is a reason for each action we take, whether we are consciously aware of the reasons we are doing them or not- even those behaviors that on the surface may seem crazy or self-defeating to us and other people.

Take, for example, a young woman named Amanda I worked with some time ago. Amanda was smart, attractive, and a hard worker. However, she felt stuck because she was in a very unhealthy relationship with her fiancé, John, over the past several years.

John had been emotionally and physically abusive toward her at times during their relationship, but for reasons unknown to her, she kept staying in the relationship. On one occasion, John had hurt her so severely she had to be hospitalized for three days. When Amanda was discharged from the hospital and returned to live with him, her friends were shocked. They could not understand her seemingly "crazy" behavior.

Amanda herself was confused why she wanted to stay with him after what he had done to her. However, I had seen victims of domestic violence return to their abusers many times before. Or, if they did leave without working on some of their underlying issues, they often wound up in a different relationship with another abusive partner, repeating the same old patterns.

For some time, Amanda worked in therapy on her fear of leaving this abusive relationship. At first she worked on her fear that he might harm her if she were to attempt to leave him. However, it was not until she also worked on her underlying fear of being alone and emotionally vulnerable, and her fear of being unable to financially support herself that she began to truly feel strong enough to take action to move on.

She came to realize her own strength and value as an individual and truly believed she was entitled to enjoy a much better life. Not long after, Amanda decided to speak to her boss and arranged to transfer her job to one of the company's branch stores in California. When Amanda moved, she left everything behind and started her life over. She even started her own business after a while, and it was a great success. She used her financial success to start a women's shelter for other abused women. Amanda had gained her own strength and freedom and was now helping others do the same.

Likewise, our continuing to smoke cigarettes that we know are harming us is just like being in an emotionally and physically abusive relationship that for some reason we just can't leave.

Almost every smoker I work with struggles to make sense of why they continue to smoke even when they know smoking is "bad" for them. They really want to quit but feel they can't for some reason. When I ask them what they enjoy most about smoking, they are usually at a loss for words. In their loss for a rational explanation, they provide a default explanation, such as, "I don't know" or "I guess I must enjoy it or I wouldn't do it, right?"

Or they say, "It's hard to describe." But if pressed for what specifically it is they enjoy about smoking, they all are at a loss for a clear and rational explanation. This does not mean they are "crazy" or confused. It just means they have yet to really understand the underlying mechanics behind why they continue to smoke and remain in an abusive relationship. When they do finally understand it, it's like they received a golden key to finally unlock the door that leads to their freedom.

Like Amanda did so successfully, we too can gain the strength to leave our abusive relationship with cigarettes behind us for good and move on to a happier and more enjoyable life. Once we overcome our fear of quitting and truly understand the purpose behind this self-defeating behavior, we can then substitute other more healthy behaviors in its place; behaviors that will be less harmful to us in the long run and make life way more pleasurable on every level!

## Symptom Substitution Isn't the Solution!

What I hope you take away from this discussion is simply that we need to better understand our fear and learn what is driving our smoking, so we can successfully satisfy that desire or drive without substituting it for yet another behavior that has an equal, or even more negative, consequence in its place. Because, I'll go out on a limb here and take a wild guess that we don't want to quit smoking today to then find ourselves compulsively overeating. Then gain weight and be 50 pounds heavier six months from now, only to be so depressed about our weight gain that we start smoking again!

This leads us directly to the second important concept to consider. Sigmund Freud, arguably the greatest explorer of the underlying mechanisms of human behavior, has *shed light on why eliminating the problem behavior alone is futile.* Why, he argued, symptom substitution would occur if you do not resolve the underlying drive.

"Symptom substitution" is the process wherein you consciously or unconsciously trade in one problem behavior for yet another. Sometimes this trade can be perceived as having been overall a good one. And that's fine. Because I am not a purest, if something works well for someone, that's great. If that person perceives themselves as better off, they probably are.

For those who don't simply want to trade in smoking for another bad habit, please keep reading. But, even for those who are okay with the trade, I suggest you keep reading as well. Just in case you change your mind somewhere down the road. As I have found, this is often exactly the case with many of the people I have come across on my journey.

## No One Is Here to Force You to Quit

By the way, a quick disclaimer: this method will not force anyone to quit against their will. When I first started to write this book: I remember many of my friends and colleagues saying, "I'm so glad you're writing this book, I can't wait to give it to my brother, husband, wife, girlfriend, best friend, etc... so I can make them quit smoking." To which they all seemed surprised when I said, "Sorry. *The Secret* is unbelievably powerful, but it can't *make* them quit smoking." After their jaw would hit the floor, they almost always followed up with, "Why not?"

You see, there are many people who actually enjoy smoking (or think they enjoy smoking) and don't want to give it up. What has been built into *The Secret* is a kind of safety mechanism that prevents other people from using its remarkable power to control someone else against their wishes.

Think about it. What if we were all in possession of a power so strong it could alter other people's behaviors that we don't personally like? That would be amazing, right? Come on, admit it. Wouldn't it be great to change some of the behaviors of the people around us? You could have your partner change those annoying behaviors like being late, insensitive, cheap, or self-centered. Or the ability to zap your kids so they clean up their toys, brush their teeth, and jump in bed before being threatened ten times. What about the ability to have your dog walk itself on a cold night? Better yet, have your boss recognize how truly valuable you are to the company and pay you what you are *really* worth!

But regrettably, its power has built-in limits.

Trust me, I've tried!

The good news is, even if you are not ready to quit smoking just yet, and you are reading this more because a loved one or friend begged you to read this, you are still in an excellent position to learn everything you eventually need to know when the day comes that you do decide to quit on your own. Nothing in this book is an attempt to trick or persuade you against your will. There are no scare tactics or hidden subliminal messages. Every thing is on the up and up.

But be warned, once you begin to see how easy it can be to quit and how truly enjoyable it is to be on the other side of the dreadful "habit," there will be a small but fast growing part of you that will begin to want to jump ship and join the countless others whose lives have been dramatically transformed by this secret.

There really is nothing to be anxious about, yet no matter how many times I try to explain this, there are still occasionally individuals who are a bit apprehensive to learn *The Secret*. Sometimes they purposefully put off reading and learning about it for months. In fact, one woman I worked with asked to have one of the very first copies of the book, and I was more than happy to give it to her. After some time had passed, I asked her what she thought about it. She looked at me somewhat hesitantly and said, "You know, I haven't even had the nerve to read it yet. It sits on my kitchen table, and I look at it every day. I really do want to read it, but I'm not ready yet."

This apprehensiveness is common. It's important to know that when you are ready, even if it's just ready to begin reading, then that in itself is part of the process. It will take some people little to almost no time to move through the book, whereas others will have to feel their way through it at their own pace.

There are no timelines and nothing to fear. What often happens is that when one eventually pushes through this initial fear, they soon find becoming a nonsmoker is one of the single most positive experiences they have ever had. The only regret they have afterward is that they wished they had not put off reading the book for so long. They almost feel cheated at having not taken the opportunity sooner. Either way, it is essential to know that you are in control of this process.

When you turn the next page, you begin the process of regaining control over your smoking and your life.

# 3

---

# THE PROMISE

This is probably a natural place for a smoke break. "What! Are you kidding me?" No. Go ahead and have a smoke. Or not. It's up you. All that is really important to know is that you can smoke whenever and wherever you want as you continue on this journey. In fact, it is essential that you continue smoking as you normally would as you read on for several important reasons. First, there is a process you will need to go through that works best if you remain smoking as usual. This process will eventually permit you to galvanize your awareness and understanding, which will eventually return you back to the natural state you were born in—as a nonsmoker.

To skip this step and hastily stop smoking cold turkey has proven for many to be disastrous. At first they feel very strong and committed to their decision to quit, and they throw their packs away. They make it through the first couple of days with little difficulty and appear to have successfully "kicked the habit."

But because they did not go through all the necessary steps to gain the important insights understood by the four percent mentioned earlier, they soon fall right back into the trap. Sometimes slowly; other times precipitously.

Secondly, unless you have already quit smoking for a while, I highly recommend you hold off doing so until after you read this entire book because the level of anxiety that can surface before one achieves a complete understanding of the process can be so distracting, and your attention won't be entirely focused on the steps discussed throughout the book. So *it is crucial for you to wait to quit smoking* until after you have gone through all the necessary steps covered in the following chapters.

## Which Cigarette Will Be Your Last?

It's probably a good idea not to put too much pressure on yourself to try to figure out which cigarette will be your very last. You see, as you read on, there may be a subtle, almost imperceptible change taking place. It will be perhaps just below your conscious radar, but it will be occurring nonetheless as you begin to learn more about *The Secret* described in this book. The answer to which cigarette will be your last will become clear to you when the time is right.

For others, the process of coming to truly know *The Secret to Stop Smoking* will be about as subtle as a freaking freight train aimed straight at them, lights beaming and whistle screeching!

That's how it was for me on my last attempt to quit smoking. It was so amazing that in the beginning I couldn't believe it. At first I didn't even recognize its true power. This amazing change didn't even register when I woke up that first morning after I quit until on my drive to work.

I looked down and noticed I had a few cigarettes that were left in the console of my car, but I had absolutely *no desire* to smoke them. No big deal, right? But in the past, when out of smokes, I always looked for that hopefully one misplaced or forgotten cigarette. That is until I could get my hands on another pack at the store.

What struck me was not this first time I saw those three cigarettes left in my car console. But it smacked me right in the face when I saw them still there a few days later and *still had no desire to smoke them.*

This had NEVER HAPPENED TO ME BEFORE. I've tried quitting before but always would smoke that last cigarette I found lying around. I would simply say to myself, "no need to waste this one." Or, "I'll just smoke this, and then it's quits for good." Of course, that one cigarette would only lead to another and another and then "to hell with it, I might as well just buy a pack." Not this time, though. Something was dramatically different, and I knew it.

Even more strange was that my mother-in-law had left an entire carton of cigarettes behind in her dash to go to the airport and not miss her plane to return back to her home in Europe. I never bought more than two or three packs at a time because, like so many smokers, it was one of the ways to try to trick myself to not smoke too much. Because I was always planning to make a break from smoking one day, but it was always one day in the distant future. Now, even with a full carton of free cigarettes on the kitchen counter, I had absolutely no desire to even have a single cigarette.

Those three little cigarettes stayed there in my car every day for weeks and the full carton stayed untouched in my kitchen too. To this very day, I still remember that day when it REALLY hit me that something had happened to me. Something unlike any time before when I tried to stop smoking but always still had those remaining unquenchable urges to light up and would give in to the urge like a weakling. Even worse than that feeling was the feeling of being *out of control*.

This time, it was very different. This time, I knew I was done for good and would never light another smoke ever again. I knew it, and you will too when it happens to you. That's A Promise!

The puzzling thing I could not figure out was why this time was so vastly different than the hundreds of other times before. Nothing seemed to have happened on the surface to make it obvious to me. I did not have a single clue. It wasn't that I had received notice of a life-threatening condition my smoking was causing that scared me to quit. It certainly wasn't that anybody threatened me with a dire consequence if I didn't quit. The price of smokes did not go up. And I didn't promise anyone else I would quit.

Then what was it? Stranger to me yet was I began feeling incredibly strong and clear in my mind, as if I had some *restored sense of control over my life*. I couldn't make sense of how a seeming miracle had occurred out of my conscious awareness that instantly freed me from my years of dreadful addiction to nicotine. But what exactly had caused this miracle did not become clear to me until much later.

As you read further along, you might be shocked to find out just what had caused this change to occur and be pleased to find out how easily it can happen for you too.

# 4

---

# HOW THE MIND WORKS

Alright, here is some good news. The very fact that you are still reading this book and you've made it this far shows you have what it takes and that there is a very strong probability you will, in fact, soon quit smoking.

Don't close the book just yet, though. We are just packing our suitcase to start the journey which will end in learning everything you absolutely need to know to stop smoking for good. It's easy... but not that easy.

## Revisit the Past to Create a More Promising Future

Let's start at the beginning. In your mind, go back to the time before you tried your very first cigarette. For some of us, this will not be too long ago; for others, it will be decades ago.

Don't just keep reading. Stop. Take a minute, and go back in time in your mind. Can you remember how old you were, where you lived, and who you lived with? As you re-experience this time, can you remember how you felt, what you looked like, what was most important in your life at that time?

Go ahead and take some time to do this exercise. I'll wait....

Did you really do the exercise? If not, why? This is an important step in re-programming your brain. *You see, you will need to literally readjust your self-concept to once again view yourself as a nonsmoker.* We all carry some very powerful self-images that, whether we are aware of them or not, greatly influence our every behavior. These self-images significantly impact our beliefs, feelings, and therefore our actions throughout the day. In fact, each morning we are literally re-programming our self-concept of how we view ourselves and the world around us.

Usually we stick to our typical and habitually way of acting and therefore have pretty similar experiences as we did the day before. However, if we really wanted to, each day we could redesign our lives. We could, in fact, recreate aspects of ourselves to not only act differently than we've been in the past, but also to *be* radically different than our pasts!

What I would like to ask you to do now is to think of the five most important characteristics or aspects about yourself that best describe who you really are. These may be five roles you engage in on a daily basis that you would use to describe yourself if you were to introduce yourself to someone you have never met before.

Often these five roles are related to our gender, whether we are married or single, our role in our family (daughter, wife, father, son, etc.), the religion we practice, and our position/status in our career or education, and so on.

Please go ahead and take a minute and write down the five most important and self-descriptive characteristics about you right here:

1) _____
2) _____
3) _____
4) _____
5) _____

Okay let's take a moment to reflect on what you just wrote. You did write them, right? If not, please stop and take the minute it takes to get a pen and do this simple exercise that can help dramatically change your life for the better. (You'll need the pen later on anyway.) Don't worry. I'll still be here when you get back.

Now, let me share something very important about this exercise: **never have I heard someone refer to themselves as a smoker in this exercise!** It's just not up there on our list of most important things in our lives. Yet, this single habit often dictates many aspects of how we spend our waking time and how other people view us. Over the next couple of days, start to take notice throughout your day how many times you engage in smoking-related thoughts and behaviors. Way too much!

This is all about to change. *Soon you will begin to focus more of your valuable time and energy on the five most important aspects of your life.* And guess what? Those areas will begin to dramatically improve (even if they are already going pretty well).

# 5

---

# WHY YOU HAVE NOT QUIT BEFORE

That which we believe to be true in our minds tends to become our reality, *if* we hold on to the thought for a long enough time.

Basically, this process, which is called a *self-fulfilling prophesy,* works like this: The thoughts and beliefs we have about a particular person, thing, or event may or may not be completely accurate, but our believing it can influence our behavior in a way that we unknowingly bring them about in our reality.

Okay that's an interesting concept, but you might be wondering why I'm telling you this. What does this have to do with your ability to quit smoking? Well, this self-fulfilling prophecy occurs on many levels and in many areas of one's life. In fact, this phenomenon occurs to practically every single person no matter how brilliant or not so brilliant they are.

For example, if you have always seen yourself as not being a very good dancer, then you will tend to avoid dancing. By avoiding dancing, you never allow yourself to start gaining skills which would actually improve your ability to dance. And by avoiding it, you miss out on the joy and rapture that happens when you dance. Thus, you are turning your beliefs into a self-perpetuating reality.

The same process holds true for your belief about whether you are a good singer or not. Notwithstanding, the exact same process holds true for your belief about being a smoker or a nonsmoker.

Now if you have been repeatedly telling yourself you're a smoker and you will always be a smoker, you are actually manifesting this belief into a reality. Fortunately, the very same process holds true if you begin to think and visualize yourself as already moving along the road toward your destination of successfully quitting and returning to your natural state of living as a nonsmoker once again.

You are probably saying, "Come on, it can't be that easy!" Well, it might just be. You won't really know until you try, right? What do you have to lose anyway by trying?

Go ahead and take a second to visualize yourself as having been a non-smoker for one year already. Come on, this will be fun. You can make this more real by visualizing your surroundings. If you're inside your home, look around the room and begin to notice all the old places you kept your lighter, matches, and cigarettes are now surprisingly void of these objects. In their place might be a vase with a fresh arrangement of white and yellow flowers. Notice how somehow even the air seems to be different. You can actually smell the flowers in that vase because your olfactory senses have been restored. In fact, the natural sunlight filling the room even seems to be brighter than usual.

Take some time to sit and let your mind begin to readjust to this new self-perception and restoration of your sensory receptors. You may even begin to feel a renewed sense of energy, excitement, and joy that hadn't been there in a long time. Hold these thoughts in your mind as if they are already happening. How do you feel now that you have purged all the toxins completely from your mind and body? Now that your body has been restored to its healthier, more energetic state?

Allow yourself to feel the energy running through your body. No longer are you ruled by uncomfortable and demanding cravings; instead you are bursting with a natural sense of stimulation and guided along by a renewed passion for activities you enjoy.

Hold these thoughts in your mind each day, and you will soon begin to see in the not-too-distant future that you no longer need to imagine this, because it will be your reality.

"See things as you would have them be instead of as they are."
-Robert Collier

Before we continue on with this journey, I have a quick reminder. Earlier on I mentioned to you there were several little known but extremely powerful and proven steps that, when used correctly, will help you quickly experience a remarkable transformation back to becoming a non-smoker again and enjoying all the benefits that come with it. I want to again emphasize the importance of keeping an open mind as you learn about these steps—even if at first some of them don't seem to be all that important or relevant. Trust me, they are.

The best analogy I can think of to explain the importance of each individual step is to compare it to the recipe printed on the back of a box of cake mix. Take Betty Crocker, for instance. Say you bought a box of this cake mix and brought it home and decided to make it.

As you read the directions, it says something like: first preheat the oven to 400 degrees. Then get a large bowl and add 2 eggs, 1 cup of milk, 1 stick of butter, and add the cake mix. Now stir all the ingredients together. Then the directions tell you to grease a pan and place the batter into the pan and cook in the oven at 400 degrees for 20 minutes or until golden brown on the top, remove, and let cool.

If, for some reason, you were out of milk or forgot to do a little step like grease the pan, your cake is going to come out very different than the one shown on the cover of the box. Each step, no matter how small, is very important. Not greasing the pan would cause the cake, even if perfectly cooked, to become stuck to the bottom of the pan and very difficult to remove without damaging the cake. Not setting the oven at the recommend temperature would cause the inside of the cake to remain gooey and uncooked, and it would not taste so great. This would not mean that Betty Crocker's recipe is wrong or doesn't work. It would instead show that each step is actually essential to follow if you want to have the rewards of a great-tasting cake.

So please keep this example in mind and stay faithful to the steps covered in here because following them will provide you with a truly amazing outcome. But... you have to follow the steps.

# 6

---

# THE SMOKER'S CLUB

You may not yet be entirely convinced that a method this powerful and easy could really exist, and that's understandable. This might be a good time to tell you more about how I first came upon such a remarkable discovery. And why I feel so strongly about its power that I want to share it with as many people as possible.

Much of my professional life has been spent in the pursuit of understanding the underlying dynamics of human behavior and working as a clinical psychologist with individuals and families to make positive changes in their lives. In my private life, I have been fortunate enough to have married a woman who became my best friend and the mother of two very remarkable kids.

Somewhere along the line, I decided to add "real-estate investor" to my repertoire. This is when my occasional cigarette smoking exploded into a full-blown smoke fest! While exciting and challenging, I was not prepared for the sheer amount of stress I was about to take on. I slowly began buying rundown properties and renovating them myself, after my day job. Then I would turn each successfully converted house's equity into yet another real-estate purchase. A lot of this work was dirty and downright disgusting, as you could not believe how many rats and cockroaches could harmoniously live in one attic.

Soon smoke breaks were a great way to put off going into the attic to make a needed repair. Or, after cleaning out a rat-infested attic, a smoke break was a great reward for my hard work. Not too much time had passed, and I had amassed literally millions of dollars worth of properties (and smoked thousands of cigarettes).

The problem was I was the landlord, landscaper, rental agent, rent collector, and responsible for paying the mortgage on all these properties. Remember, this was my part-time job!

Each successive responsibility brought with it added stress, and I soon found solace in the group of smokers at my day job. The Smoker's Club. What a comforting place this can be. Everyone is friendly and supportive. They too have much stress and work and are always looking for a break from it all. This was my crowd. My home away from home, if you will.

As you likely know, there's a smoker's club practically everywhere you go. You find them at work, weddings, bars, training conventions, malls, parks, and even little kids' birthday parties! Once you're inducted and given membership into the smoker's club, you are given a lifetime pass. No membership fees apply. All you have to do is bring your smokes, and you don't even have to do that all the time, as members will always share. In fact, bumming a smoke can even lead to new friendships. Who would want to leave this place?

Great as this place seemed, every once in a while, a defection would occur by one of the members. Not often, but it would happen. Once a very good friend of mine, Gary, an older gentleman who I thought started the original smoker's club at the office, all of a sudden stopped showing up. He had been a two-pack-a-day smoker for most of his life. Now, after decades of smoking, he had a chart marking his "days clean" on his office wall calendar. He was a bit of a celebrity around the building. He even got a party to celebrate his six months clean by the non-smokers at work. This is one of the influential events that helped spark my curiosity, which would eventually grow into a full-blown investigation of why and how some people are able to "give up" smoking while most others struggle and rarely succeed.

Another interesting thing occurred to my friend Gary after he quit. He slowly started to resemble Santa Claus as he packed on pound after pound. And just in time as the holiday decorations and parties were beginning to appear around our building. Needless to say, the smokers weren't as impressed as the non-smokers were with Gary's BIG *transformation*. We'll get back to my friend's motivation to quit and subsequent weight gain a little later on as he helped lead me to uncover one of the most crucial insights needed to uncovering *The Secret to Stop Smoking,* **without gaining weight** or any other unwanted side effects.

# 7

## NICOTINE: MORE ADDICTIVE THAN CRACK COCAINE?

The reason most people keep smoking even when they say they really don't want to often can be one of the most puzzling things for people to understand.

This has led to a commonly held belief that smoking cigarettes is more addictive than heroin. This is a common misperception. In fact, nicotine is *not* more addictive than heroin or crack cocaine. What is true is because of the way in which nicotine enters the body, via smoking, it is amazingly fast to register in the receptors in our brains. In fact, it takes nicotine just three seconds to register in our brain cells.

I had always assumed that a junkie injecting heroin directly into his veins via a hypodermic needle was experiencing the fastest rush possible on earth, yet it is the nicotine junkie that does!

**As powerful and fast as the nicotine rush is, the physical withdrawal symptoms from quitting nicotine are only about as strong as the withdrawal symptoms average coffee drinkers experience when they stop their caffeine intake suddenly.**

After a day or two, the discomfort is practically unnoticeable. In fact, for most people, the nicotine withdrawal symptoms are practically undetectable. To prove this phenomenon, you need just look at how most expectant mothers can quit smoking on the day they learn they are pregnant with no problems or cravings.

Or, how the lifelong two-pack-a-day smoker can immediately quit smoking cold turkey once they learn they have a life-threatening illness. **Without the aid of a single nicotine replacement treatment!**

### Crazy Additive? Or Not?

How can this be? Nicotine is supposed to be crazy addictive? If it isn't, then why has it been so darn hard to quit before?

The great pain and difficulty of overcoming addiction to nicotine is a common myth perpetuated by those in the pharmaceutical industry as well as the stop-smoking products industry. Now to some this may sound like complete nonsense. Why in the world would the anti-smoking products industry exaggerate the addictive nature of nicotine and overplay the discomfort of the detoxification period once you quit smoking?

Believe it or not, it's for the same reason that the tobacco companies underplay it. Money! Money! Money! Lots and lots of it!

Just think about it. If you believe cigarettes are the most addictive drug on the planet earth and that quitting "cold turkey" will be as painful as having all of your teeth pulled out one by one with a pair of rusty old pliers, then you will spend any amount of money to purchase the latest product that promised to help make this process less painful and could help you get over the "severe" addiction to nicotine.

And guess what? When you run out of this magic product or when the latest high-tech procedure ultimately ends up as a "relapse," you just need to *buy* more of their product or gadget!

The nicotine patch, gum, and inhaler are all simply substitute ways of maintaining your body's supply of nicotine. Eventually, when you stop the product, you experience the withdrawal symptoms.

### The True Level of Discomfort

The good news is that while you may still have to experience some form of physical discomfort when you quit, the degree of discomfort is nowhere near as bad as we have been led to believe. Many have likened this detoxification process to be similar to the symptoms experienced from the common cold. And we have all survived the common cold.

Of equal importance is that these nicotine replacement methods are not how the majority of successful individuals actually stop smoking over a long period of time.

Don't just take my word for it. Do a little research. Take a second to go on the internet and put the words "stop smoking independent research results" in the search browser and see what you find.

Independent studies (those not paid for by the makers of the products) have consistently shown that over 90% of the people who have successfully quit smoking cigarettes for more than one year did so without the aid of any of these devices. This trend is even more noticeable in studies which are conducted over even longer periods of time and employ multiple follow-up investigations.

Why is this?

## Your Psychological Dependence

The answer is simple. More powerful than the physical dependence on nicotine is the psychological dependence on smoking cigarettes. In other words, the reasons we tell ourselves why we continue to smoke. This powerful aspect will not be overcome by any of the products mentioned above. They simply address the physical aspects, *not* the psychological ones. Until the psychological dependence is understood and is removed, there can be no moving on.

**The physical dependence on nicotine is responsible for less than 20 percent of the addictive nature of cigarettes, whereas the psychological dependence accounts for more than 80 percent of the addiction.**

If this is not addressed, it can be a life of thinking of cigarettes and missing them. *This missing or the urge to have another cigarette is what causes the majority of individuals to relapse.*

I have heard so many people who use nicotine replacement therapy or willpower alone methods of quitting complain about constantly thinking and dreaming about having a smoke, even after they have quit smoking for months or even years. This is not the method I recommend. The good news is this is <u>not </u>what happens when you follow the simple steps discussed in this book. It will actually be the exact opposite. You will feel relieved. You will have the feeling that you would rather be punched in the face than smoke another cigarette again.

The smell of smoke will cause you, as it did when you were originally a non-smoker, to turn and walk away from other smokers still caught in the trap. The smell of smoke will be anything but nostalgic. You will feel only elation that you are free from the horrible nightmare and feel sympathy for those still stuck in its evil grip.

In fact, once you learn and implement *The Secret,* it will be hard for you to keep yourself from going out and telling every smoker you encounter just how easy it is to quit and to please stop harming themselves.

So from here on out, the majority of our focus will be on the 80 percent of the addiction, since removing the psychological dependence on cigarettes is the biggest problem most people struggle with to quit for good.

The following chapter will cover the main reasons or beliefs most people give for why they continue to smoke. Most people will freely acknowledge smoking is not healthy for them and explain they are planning to quit some day soon. Usually about six months from any given day you ask them. **What is helpful then is to systematically explore the reasons you tell yourself why you continue to smoke.**

> "Now the general who wins a battle makes many calculations in his temple ere the battle is fought. The general who loses the battle makes but few calculations beforehand. Thus do many calculations beforehand lead to victory, and few calculations to defeat."
>
> -Sun Tzu, *The Art of War*

# 8

---

# GREAT MYTHS ABOUT SMOKING

"All power is from within and therefore under our control."

-Robert Collier

You have the power at any time to stop reading this book. You could "accidentally" misplace this book, or purposefully never pick it up again. Right now you could even throw this book across the room! I've actually done this once or twice before with my painfully boring "required" textbooks in graduate school.

Clearly if you are reading this far, you have a true desire to stop smoking and are looking for the best way to accomplish this. You know this is *possible*, but you need some guidance to get there. This is not unlike how I know it's possible to get in my car and drive to Disney World from my house in Fort Lauderdale. Yet I wouldn't just jump in my car without a credible map showing me what roads to take to get there, or I might just end up in Key West.

Not all roads lead to Disney, and not all approaches to stop smoking lead to lasting success!

What I have found through my interviews with hundreds of successful ex-smokers, and what ultimately was the key to my ability to break free of the desire to smoke, will be laid out in specific and concrete detail as you read on. **Knowing the secret to other's success is like having a detailed map to get you someplace you've never been before but really want to go.**

First, it will be helpful to find out why you have had such difficulty quitting in the first place. You see, understanding why you continue to smoke is extremely important. As with driving on a trip, it is as important to know when you are going in the *wrong* direction as it is to know when you are heading in the *right* direction.

Let's look at a couple of the things you are likely telling yourself that lead you to think you actually "enjoy" smoking:

## MYTH #1 -"SMOKING HELPS ME RELAX."

Does inhaling on a cigarette actually help one relax? I had always thought this was true. Behavioral psychologists have long shown that simply taking a long, deep breath and holding it in, then slowly releasing it is a highly effective way to reduce stress and anxiety. Breathing exercises have long been prescribed by psychotherapists to their clients' who suffer from post-traumatic stress disorder (PTSD), especially when the exercise is paired with recurring traumatic images or "flashbacks." This technique has helped thousands who suffer from panic attacks and social phobias as well. So maybe there's some truth that smoking cigarettes are a way to reduce stress?

While the act of taking long, deep breaths is stress reducing and can lower your heart rate, the act of inhaling cigarette smoke and the carcinogens it contains does not have this stress-reducing effect on the body. In fact, cigarette smoking increases one's heart rate.

What appears to happen instead is that when we start to become stressed, we search for a way to lower this growing discomfort. We fantasize that if we only had a smoke, we could start to lower this stress. When we go take a cigarette break we typically remove ourselves from the anxiety-provoking thoughts or situation when we go to smoke.

What happens next is that we are actually distracting ourselves from this noxious stimulus. The act of distraction is probably more influential in any lowering of stress, if this in fact occurs at all.

One could equally reduce stress by taking a break and walking around the block or by playing a video game and have the exact same impact. What happens in both cases is that whether we distract ourselves through a smoke, by taking a walk, listening to a song or whatever, when we return to the problem or situation, it is still there. But we are somewhat removed from the intensity of the thoughts and feelings we were experiencing about them. Needless to say, nothing has really changed, except our perception.

What is important to take away from this isn't so much that smoking doesn't truly relax us as much as it *distracts us*.

For instance, think of how you get a strong urge to smoke the more you experience stress. Obvious yes, but it's extremely important to remain mindful as you begin to more closely scrutinize this phenomenon over the next few days. I often watch this exact phenomenon occur with the students I teach at the University, especially on the day of an exam. You can find the students puffing away before class, right up until the last minute before the class starts. The stronger the stress level, the greater the urge to smoke.

The good news here is that one could just as easily skip the cigarette and do the deep breathing exercises. It's healthier, cheaper, and more effective. What I do, especially before big seminars where I speak in front of large groups of people I've never met before, is use my Ipod with my favorite music that inspires me. Or I listen to a motivational speaker to help immediately break me out of a funk. I highly recommend listening to any audio recording by Anthony Robbins, Les Brown, or Zig Ziglar. You cannot listen to them and stay stressed out, stuck, or depressed for too long!

These methods can help quickly change your mood. With the advent of digital music and small devices to play all your favorite music and recordings anywhere and anytime, this is a great alternative way to alter your mood without harming your body. Try it!

"The more we change the way we look at things, the more the things we look at change."

-Dr. Wayne Dyer

## MYTH #2 -"I CAN QUIT ANYTIME I WANT TO."

Some smokers will tell you they enjoy smoking, but if for some reason they ever felt like not smoking in the future, they could easily quit on their own. This is an interesting statement because it is difficult to prove or disprove since it is always suggested as occurring sometime in the future and, therefore, not subject to any form of immediate validation.

I truly believe that in their minds, these smokers are 100% sincere. There are even some occasional smokers who have not yet established a true addiction or dependence to cigarettes who may be accurate in their belief that they can quit if and when they want. But given enough repeated exposure to nicotine, they too will eventually lose this ability. **It is a slow yet *inevitable* process that as the body and mind are repeatedly exposed to nicotine, the body begins to habituate and attempts to maintain a steady level of nicotine in the blood.**

Each time a smoker takes another cigarette, she unknowingly re-establishes the entire nicotine-withdrawal-replenishment cycle. The discomfort from the withdraw phase of this cycle, though rather mild, is still strong enough to eventually wear down the individual to give-in and replenish the supply of nicotine the body has grown accustomed to and now craves.

As noted earlier, the physical dependence is relatively minor in comparison to the psychological dependence. So once a person gives in and takes a single dose of nicotine into his system to avoid the physical discomfort, it not only starts the physical dependence all over again but also jumpstarts the psychological cravings that must be constantly fed as well.

This is the vicious cycle that inevitably overcomes every smoker, even the occasional smoker, and after many repeated failed attempts to quit smoking, it leads straight to the construction of an unconscious psychological defense mechanism that deceives the smoker into thinking he or she actually *enjoys* smoking and is *in control* of the intake.

In reality, we are anything but in control. We are at the whim of the nicotine tyrant who constantly dictates when it is feeding time. Ever notice that the average smoker smokes about a pack of cigarettes a day. There are 20 cigarettes in a pack, and this is not by any random design of the tobacco companies. Nor is it done by accident. It is very much intentional.

Because nicotine is broken down in half by the body within one to two hours, the average smoker tends to have an urge for a cigarette about every hour or two. The pack design permits a steady dose to maintain the nicotine throughout the day. Think about this for a minute. Have you ever been late to an appointment because you had to have your smoke first? Or, have you ever sat outside in the freezing snow or rain to have a cigarette (because you enjoy it so much)?

Why is it for most smokers, we have a smoke immediately before going to bed for the night and then almost immediately after waking up in the morning–every night and every morning without fail? Is this really by choice? I love chocolate cake, but I don't have a piece of cake every night before bed and every morning when I wake up, for the rest of my life.

In my case, it was standing in the blazing hot Florida sun in the 95-degree heat in a long-sleeved shirt and tie, sweating with my work buddies. All of us sweating so we could get our nicotine fix. Why would any of us not wait to smoke until a later time when we wouldn't be late or in such miserable weather conditions if we were in control of our smoking?

Why? *Because we are not in control.*

We are feeding the nicotine tyrant who doesn't care how hot, cold, or wet it is outside, or what harm we do to our bodies. The nicotine tyrant demands ultimate control and dictates where and when it's time to smoke, not the other way around.

"In mind as in matter, in thoughts as in things, in deeds as in natural processes, there is a fixed foundation of law which, if consciously or ignorantly ignored, leads to disaster and defeat. It is, indeed, the ignorant violation of this law which is the cause of the world's pain and sorrow."

- James Allen

## MYTH #3 -"I'LL QUIT IN A LITTLE WHILE…"

Sir Isaac Newton's First Law of Motion states: "An object in motion tends to stay in motion with the same speed and in the same direction unless acted upon by an outside force."

In other words, people keep on doing what they are doing unless something stronger causes them to stop. This natural tendency for people to resist change in their present state of motion has been labeled by scientists as *inertia*. This can best explain why people who are nonsmokers tend to remain nonsmokers throughout their entire lives, and likewise why the majority of smokers continue to smoke unless somehow they learn the secret to overcoming the powerful forces of nicotine addiction already set in motion.

Prior to Newton's revelation of the Law of Motion, the dominant thought throughout the world was that it was the tendency of objects in motion to come to a natural resting position on their own. In this fashion, people commonly believed an object in motion needed an additional force to keep pushing it forward or else it would simply stop by itself.

Newton found that moving objects eventually stop *only* because of an opposing force, which has since been termed friction. He further postulated that if friction (such as gravity and/or wind resistance) could be completely removed, the object would continue moving forward indefinitely. Newton built on Galileo's concepts by arguing that a force is not needed to keep an object in motion; instead a force is needed to stop it from continuing its forward motion.

You might be wondering what all this talk about gravity, inertia, and friction has to do with you. These are important concepts to keep in mind on your way to becoming a nonsmoker again, because the very same Natural Laws described above apply to breaking free from smoking. Without a sufficient degree of force, the smoker will continue her patterned behavior of smoking indefinitely. Smokers will typically say they are going to quit someday. Just not today. It is truly their belief and intention that one day they will just decide that they have outgrown the desire to smoke and then they will move on from their unhealthy addiction.

What is not fully understood by most smokers is just how Newton's Law of Motion directly applies to the dreadful nicotine addiction too. There is a lack of appreciation of just how much direct and purposeful force will need to be summoned by the smoker to eventually overcome the momentum of the addiction already set in motion for so many years. Given this new appreciation and awareness of just how this process works, what do you think it will take for you to overcome your inertia?

LAW #2: **Without a stronger degree of opposing force, the smoker will continue her patterned behavior of smoking indefinitely.**

"One might as well try to ride two horses moving in different directions, as to try to maintain in equal force two opposing or contradictory sets of desires."

- Robert Collier

## MYTH #4 –"IF I QUIT, I'LL GAIN WEIGHT…"

This one myth can be quite easily disproven by simply looking at the fact that there are in fact some overweight smokers. Cigarettes can suppress your appetite for a short time after you smoke. However, people can and do actually gain weight later on in the evening and at night when their appetites come back.

At these times, they tend to make up for their lack of food intake by binging on high-caloric foods, which more than compensates for the reduced quantity of food intake during the earlier parts of the day. In general, it's not the amount of food that causes weight gain but instead the type of foods we eat.

Immediately after one stops smoking, some people will notice a drop in their sugar levels and a small increase in appetite for the first day or two. This is largely due to their bodies trying to readjust back to their normal states. In attempt to cope with this drop in sugar levels, most people start eating large amounts of junk food like chocolate or doughnuts and such, but it takes a long time for the body to break down these foods and then transfer them throughout the body.

A better way to cope with this short time period is to drink plenty of fruit juice as it will more quickly restore the sugar your body is craving. Then drink plenty of water.

# 9

## WHEN IS THE SOLUTION REALLY THE PROBLEM?

Here is something I couldn't quite figure out for a while that perhaps has also happened to you before. I always thought I enjoyed smoking. In my mind, smoking wasn't the problem. It was something I looked forward to in an effort to forget my problems. So if this were true, why would I ever want to quit doing something I actually liked to do and that helped me relax?

However, every now and then, I would get sick and not feel too well, often because my immune system was constantly being rundown by all my smoking. I would get a sore throat or a sinus infection, and my body would start to feel beat up. It was during these times I thought I should probably not smoke until I felt a little better. Yet for some reason, even though I wanted to not smoke–it was just for this short period until I started feeling better after all–I kept feeling an overwhelming urge to smoke. Nine times out of ten, I would give in to the urge and have a cigarette and then feel much worse afterward.

### Why Would I Continue to Do Something I Really Didn't Want to Do?

This is where one of the very first clues emerged that there might be something going on, and I was not fully aware. Why would I continue to do something when I really didn't want to do it? Let me put it another way: why was I continuing to smoke when I knew doing so would prolong my cold and contribute to feeling worse than I was already feeling? This did not make any sense.

I thought to myself, there are a heck of a lot of things I truly enjoy doing but I don't feel compelled to do them even when I'm sick. Especially if doing them will make me feel even worse after I do them.

For instance, I now really enjoy jogging, but one time when I cut my heel, it hurt when I tried to put on my running shoes. Since it hurt to even try to put the shoe on, I just waited until it healed. I didn't feel compelled to go jogging anyway because I knew if I did my foot would only hurt worse and take much longer to heal.

So why is it we feel compelled to smoke even when there are times we might not particularly be in the mood for one or when we are not feeling well? How many other times in our lives do we act like that? I couldn't really think of any. Can you?

## Obsessing Over Cigarettes

Here is another thing I tried to figure out. Why if we run out of cigarettes, do we become so obsessed with finding one and can't think of anything else? There have been more times than I care to admit when I rummaged through my house looking for a cigarette in utter desperation. I recall many times when my kids were still young enough that they took naps in the afternoon for an hour or two. On the occasions when I would run out of cigarettes while they were sleeping, I didn't want to wake them up to go to the store, so I would go increasingly mad rummaging through the cabinets and drawers, in the garage or in the car, with the hopes of finding just one stray cigarette.

I'm sure you have had similar experiences. I remember vividly a sense of panic beginning to set in as I would start looking outside in some of my favorite smoking areas in the back garden for an old cigarette butt that had a little tobacco left in it. More times than I would like to admit, I would pick half smoked butts off the ground in my garden and smoke them to avoid waking my kids from their naps to get my nicotine fix.

I know I am not alone in this experience as I have come across many friends in this position where they were so relieved to see me, knowing I always had smokes on me, so they could bum one and get their fix.

These feelings of panic would never last very long. Often my wife would return with cigarettes, or I could easily run to the local store. But herein were the brief glimpses we all have into the growing realization in the back of our minds that we are really not in control of ourselves. This was something I wouldn't even dare look into for very long. Instead, I tried to push it off and move on.

Contemplate for a moment, if you will, why we feel a sense of panic or fear over not having access to a cigarette. Why is it practically impossible to go to sleep each night without at least one or two cigarettes on us for the morning smoke? Even if we are very hungry, we don't experience panic in a restaurant when the waiter is late bringing our food to the table. So why then do we get so darn crazy when we can't have a cigarette?

So now, consider whether you tell yourself you "enjoy" smoking sometimes to cover up an underlying fear of facing that awareness in the back of your mind that you are really just trying to avoid that sense of panic setting in if you were not to give in to the urge to smoke. How different is this really from the panic drug addicts on the street experience when they are out of money and out of drugs? Isn't it probably the exact same feeling and dire compulsion to get a fix the drug addict on the street goes through when looking to score his next fix of heroin or cocaine?

## Experience Not Smoking with Little to No Panic or Discomfort?

Now for the good news, as uncomfortable as we imagine it will be to go through the withdrawal from smoking, the fear is unfounded and magnified a hundred times by our own imaginations.

The majority of people who successfully quit using *The Secret* experience almost no discomfort or panic whatsoever. In fact, they experience the exact opposite.

They feel a sense of joy and freedom as they come to a realization that they are not really being deprived of anything at all. They are actually looking forward to regaining their freedom and feel only joy and elation as they become nonsmokers once again.

And you will too. You will begin to see that leaving behind this self-imposed prison will be one of the most enjoyable things you have ever done.

# 10

## THE MILLION-DOLLAR LESSON

This may just be *THE SINGLE MOST IMPORTANT SECRET* to be revealed yet. This secret is so powerful I believe when correctly applied, it will ultimately be one of the main insights responsible for helping completely remove any urge in you to ever smoke a single cigarette again! Period. No exception.

What could be this powerful to overcome something as strong as the psychological pull of cigarettes? Well, when you hear it, you might be surprised how obvious and simple this one thing appears to be. As you read further, don't let the apparent simplicity of this phenomenon detract from its truly remarkable power.

What is even better is this simple insight can be used for achieving practically anything you want in your life, not just becoming a nonsmoker. It could easily be used to lose weight, stop drinking, stop gambling, improve your marriage, get a new career, or even make more money. Its power has no limit. The only limits that can exist are the ones placed on it.

Now this may sound too good to be true. Or, you could be thinking, "Tell me this darn secret already!" I can promise you it is not too good to be true, and I also promise I will tell you everything I have learned about this remarkable discovery. But first I'd like to share a very personal story about arguably the lowest point in my life.

### My Financial Butt Kicking

Earlier I mentioned I had been extremely stressed trying to keep my day job while managing a growing real-estate portfolio. Well, I had no idea what stress really was yet. The real-estate market was about to take the biggest plunge in value in over 25 years. In 12 months, the value of all the properties in South Florida, where I live, dropped a staggering *30 percent*. Now on one property that hurts, but on seven properties that downright stings! This drop continued for three straight years.

Imagine watching all your hard work over the past seven years begin to evaporate into nothing.

Now if I had been smoking a lot of cigarettes before the real-estate market dropped, you can only imagine how my chain smoking exploded after it. Not to mention that this sharp decline in home values would continue for three straight years. I've heard it said many times before that earning your first million dollars is the hardest, but I think *losing your first million* is way harder!

Well, losing that money was distressing, but I had also borrowed a great deal of money from family, friends, and credit cards. Not only had I lost well over a million dollars, I also owed hundreds of thousands of dollars to creditors. The people who lent me the money didn't really care about the real-estate market troubles. They wanted their money back. This was truly depressing. I had never been in this position before in my life. And, if you have been in this position, you know owing money to people you love and care about and not being able to repay them is awful. Plus, not being able to provide security for your family is nothing short of gut-wrenching. I was miserable to say the least.

But as fate would have it, out of this most trying and depressing time, something quite *extraordinary* and *priceless* would emerge.

Okay, what good could possibly come from a financial butt kicking so bad I lost over a million dollars and was now hundreds of thousands of dollars in growing debt? This debt was so enormous it almost landed me, my wife, and our two young kids homeless. We were receiving foreclosure notices on several of our properties, and it was only a matter of time before the very house we lived in was lost to foreclosure as well. Well, there comes a point when things actually get so bad that the worst possible case scenario you can imagine actually starts to be a looming near certainty.

Yet in this most out of control and stressed-out state, a small but growing realization began to emerge from seemingly out of nowhere.

## Finding Control in Complete Chaos

It became evident that I had little control over the collapsing real-estate market. I looked around and found that many of the things I was attempting to change *were completely out of my control.* This realization of my "powerlessness" at first was anything but "empowering." But because of this predicament, I started to have a clearer sense of the things that were actually *in my control.* Then I looked around and found whether we were wealthy or poor, my kids simply wanted me to put them on my shoulders and carry them to the park and play with them.

*Hey,* wait a minute, this is *in my control*!

Yet I could still hear myself saying to them, "Hold on, let me finish this cigarette, and I'll take you to the park." After the cigarette, I would have to take even more time as I would feel fatigued right after. "Hold on, give me a few minutes to rest, and then I'll take you," I'd say to them. Some times they would get tired of waiting for me to regain my energy, and they would go play on their own.

Slowly this process repeated itself many times until it finally hit me that if I really want to spend time with my kids, I might have to slow the smoking down. This thought, while motivating, had little effect on the quantity of my smoking. See, I hadn't learned *The Secret* yet, let alone begun applying its amazing power in my life.

## The Most Important Question

I can't say I remember when or where the thought first started to present itself, but clear as day, one thought began playing over and over in my head. The thought was, "**What's more important**: My health and spending quality time with my kids or having a cigarette?"

At first I would just push the thought away. But slowly over time, I started to answer myself back, "My kids and my health are *way* more important than the cigarette." The more I said this in my mind, the stronger the conviction became.

From then on, every time I had an urge to smoke, that simple thought would emerge. I could hear it again and again "**What's more important**, your kids and your health or having a smoke that really doesn't do anything for you."

If you don't have kids, don't worry. The powerful reasons for you may be different. No one can tell you exactly what your important reasons will be. You will, however, begin to find them on your own as you do the simple steps covered over the next few chapters and focus on improving the five most important aspects of your life you wrote in the earlier exercise in Chapter 3.

While I mentioned I had no control over when the real-estate market would make a rebound (if ever), there was a growing realization taking place inside me that I did have control over some other areas of my life.

Over the next few days and weeks, I began examining just how many things in my life I was stressing myself out about, but regardless how much mental energy I had put into, I HAD ABSOLUTELY NO CONTROL OVER changing them.

As you might imagine, there was a reluctance of letting go of my beliefs that I could *force* a change in some of these things. As I slowly started to let go of wanting to change other people and situations, a rush of calmness and peacefulness flooded over me. I began to start to feel less burdened by this constant battle with the world–a losing battle I had been engaged in for some time that was taking so much energy and time from my life.

It was because I began to allow myself to see more clearly the many things I had absolutely no control over that I was also gaining the ability to see how many things I actually DID HAVE CONTROL OVER! In fact, no one else had control over some of these things EXCEPT ME! The trick was to start focusing on these things and less on the ones that were out of my control.

## Thoughts Beget Actions

I told you it would sound simple. But learning how to do this takes some practice and a firm commitment to diligently focus on your thoughts.

One of the very first areas I focused my attention on was noticing that I did have a choice of whether or not I took a cigarette out of the pack and held it to my mouth and lit it. I began noticing I had really been making the decision to smoke in my mind way before I even started to take any physical action. I focused more closely at how I had created an almost delusional belief that smoking would relax me and somehow magically remove some of my stress.

I also began to see that once I had allowed myself to even think about a cigarette, this began an almost unstoppable chain of urges to go smoke. My body practically went on autopilot to get a cigarette at these times, and each time I allowed my mind to wander back to the false promise that smoking could relieve my stress.

As you may already know, cigarettes have no power to control other people or situations and, therefore, don't really have any power to remove stress *whatsoever!*

I learned that the instant I began *thinking of a cigarette* was the key time to most easily stop myself from ever actually taking a smoke. I simply reminded myself that smoking does not relieve my stress but only makes it worse. I started to remind myself that while I had little control over many of the things that upset me and I stressed about, I did have control over whether I smoked or not. As I repeated these thoughts over and over, the urge to smoke would leave as quickly as they came.

You will find in time as you implement this strategy being discussed that when your thoughts *or urge* to smoke occur, they will soon leave as quickly as they came. In time these thoughts will begin to show up in your mind less and less often as you follow these simple steps.

I share this story about possibly the worst period in my life for several reasons, all of which should be helpful for you to begin to better understand just how easy it will be for you to stop smoking, and how much more pleasurable it will be afterwards. Also, after I successfully applied the secret to finally and forever stop smoking, I realized I could use it to improve other areas of my life, and I did just that.

I soon began to have a remarkable degree of success in not only improving my health but dramatically improving my wealth! This happens because *The Secret* reveals that all areas of your life are connected to one another, so positive change in one area can, and often does, lead to change in other areas of your life.

First, I bet you can easily think of several things going on around you at this very moment that you are putting significant mental energy into and are attempting to influence the outcome. For example, it might be that you are focusing your energy on how someone is not treating you the way you would like, or how others are not making choices in their lives the way you wish they would. Or, perhaps you are focused on figuring out when the economy will make a turn for the better. Now, take a second to consider these problems. How many of these problems, no matter how much energy and time you invest in them, can you change the outcome by worrying about them?

Whenever we are focusing our attention on changing things outside of us rather than focusing on ourselves, we are setting ourselves up for feelings of disappointment, frustration, and failure. Yet by simply changing the way you look at your role in what you *can personally influence* in regard to the problem, you can greatly reduce the amount of stress you experience.

This sounds simple, but it's not always easy to do. Is it worth it? Absolutely!

## An Internal Locus of Control

This is primarily achieved by taking personal responsibility only for what is actually in your control. This is often called possessing an "internal" rather than "external" locus of control. As you likely know, the only things that are ever truly in our control are our own thoughts, beliefs, and actions! It is by redirecting our efforts on changing our own thoughts, behaviors, and actions that we can become 1,000 times more powerful!

Let me say it again: by looking at what is truly in our control (our perceptions of our problems and how we consequently feel and then act), we begin to gain the power to not only solve any problem but also to feel dramatically better over the course of our lifetimes.

In fact, most people struggle to find what they truly want in LIFE simply because they are looking for it in all the wrong places. By simply shifting from an external focus to an internal focus you begin to find that which you seek you already possess.

**The Paradox of Life...as soon as you give up trying to control everything... is the moment you begin to be more in control.**

Second, this million-dollar example destroys the common myth that the best time to attempt to quit smoking is when you have very little stress.

This is a trap! There will never be a time in your life when you are stress-free. More importantly, *this is just another way to give up control in your life.*

You see, by waiting for some external relief of stress, you lose control over your future! You have little impact on many things outside yourself. If you wait for life to get easier, you will be waiting forever.

As further evidence of the importance of not letting outside events determine when you will quit, please consider this: not long after the real-estate market collapsed, the stock market collapsed along with the world-wide banking system in practically every country on the planet. If I had been waiting for better financial times, I would still be smoking, and you would not be reading this book.

> "When we are no longer able to change a situation- we are challenged to change ourselves."
>
> - Victor Frankl

# PART TWO

# 11

## CHANGE YOUR THOUGHTS, CHANGE YOUR FUTURE

Everyone I have ever met has a DREAM—a specific vision of how they would want their lives to be if they could be dramatically different from the way they currently are now.

This ideal life would be better and more exciting. Each day would be spent doing more, having more, feeling better, and living life more passionately.

Sometimes it takes some time for them to get in touch with this ideal dream image to be able to put it into words. Often this is because they have put it far off in the back recesses of their minds and long since forgotten about it. If they take the time to look, they *always* find it is there, looming just below the surface, waiting to emerge.

For example, one woman I worked with wished she could quit her job and work in an entirely different line of work. She dreamed of moving to a small town in North Carolina and buying the house of her dreams for herself and her young daughter.

Another man wanted to eventually get the nerve up to start his own gourmet restaurant, and then later have a chain of several of these restaurants across the country.

Yet another woman had the desire to start a charity to help the poor and deprived children living in her home country of Haiti. Her desire was to help the children there who often live without the hope of a brighter future because of their impoverished circumstances and lack of educational resources.

One man intensely desired to meet and fall in love with the woman of his dreams.

One thing most of these individuals have in common is the desire to live a more meaningful, satisfying, and enriching life. Another thing some of them have in common is a belief that their dream, if even possible, is far off in the distant future. Many even have a long list of why their dream just isn't possible at this specific moment in time.

Now here is the interesting part of the equation: when I ask each one of them if they are currently taking specific steps toward making their dreams a reality, they often provide several reasons for why "right now" is not really a good time to start going after their ideal life.

Usually they are very legitimate and practical reasons, such as: "I need to work to pay the mortgage." "Where would I get the time or money to go back to college?" "After working all day long, I'm too exhausted." Or, "I'm too old."

Yet if they challenged themselves, they could find several hours a week that they currently squander watching television, going to the movies, or gossiping with others and use that time and energy instead to invest in their ideal future.

Here's the crazy part! First, I ask them to imagine that right this minute a CEO of a multi-billion dollar corporation walks in my office and hands them a guaranteed signed contract which will pay them one million dollars upon the completion of their goal. I further explain this money is already sitting in an escrow account, set aside with their name on it, waiting to be instantly transferred into their personal bank account. I ask them if this was actually happening right now, would they still feel all the reasons they gave me before for what had been holding them back would continue to exist for them.

*If they did have this absolute guarantee to be rewarded for pursuing their dream, would they immediately start going after their dream full-throttle right now?*

Their eyes always light up BIG and they say, "Of course," "Absolutely!"

Now here's the catch: life doesn't work that way. At least very rarely does something like that happen.

But what could happen is, if you could feel that internal sense of absolute confidence and hold your dream in the forefront of your mind as *the sin-*

*gle most important thought on your mind throughout the day*, your subconscious would not let anything, I repeat anything, get in your way to prevent you from reaching your goal.

Jack Canfield, Coauthor of *Chicken Soup for The Soul*, often describes this process as that of structural tension; whereby the brain has been wired in such a way that it works tirelessly day and night to ensure it creates in the real world a perfect match to the image of your dream you faithfully hold on to and believe in your own mind. This naturally occurring phenomenon is known as the Law of Attraction.

You attract into your life that which you think about most often. If you think about fear and lack of money, you become fearful and broke. (Trust me, I've seen this one play out in my own life.) If you focus on ways of earning money and obtaining success, you bring about prosperity and wealth in your life.

## The Law of Attraction in Action

Let me share a quick story that happened to me a short while ago to better demonstrate the true power of the Law of Attraction to bring into our lives that which we desire and believe in wholeheartedly.

As I mentioned earlier on, I was overwhelmed with my growing financial debt and was constantly worrying I would someday soon wind up living on the streets with no way to provide for my family. I often couldn't sleep at night because of the intense stress and pressure of my depreciating real-estate investments, so much so I wound up having my first panic attack.

Let me describe a panic attack for those of you who have been fortunate enough to never have had one before: it feels like the entire earth is moving beneath your feet and is about to open up and swallow you alive. It's unsettling to say the very least. This was the worst experience I've ever had, outside of being in a real earthquake in Los Angeles 15 years ago.

One night I finally got to a point where I screamed out loud to myself, "ENOUGH ALREADY!" Because I started to realize the more I kept thinking of all the bad things that could happen, the worse things actually got in my life, and the worse I kept feeling. I screamed, "NO MORE!"

I started to literally talk to myself out loud and repeat over and over, "Things will get better." At first I felt like I was lying to myself, but after a while, I started to really believe that things *could get better*. I was starting to be open to the possibility of money coming back into my life someday, even though I was not sure exactly how.

And I finally said to myself, "I can and will handle whatever happens, and my family and I will be okay."

A few days later, I went to a garage sale with my kids. I saw a dusty but interesting looking painting which instantly caught my eye. My kids wanted a stuffed animal and a video that was about one dollar. For some reason, I decided, even though I was broke, I should buy this old painting because I had a funny feeling in my gut it was valuable.

The homeowner was selling it for $100. I thought even if its not worth much, I could hang it in my office because it was so peaceful looking it might just help relieve some of my clients' stress... or maybe even some of my own. When I got home with this rather large painting, my wife was curious who the artist was and did a quick search online.

We were shocked when we learned it was painted by one of the greatest Vietnamese painters, Vu Cao Dam, who had recently passed away. His paintings were in rather high demand for their beauty and scarcity. Believe or not, we later sold the $100 painting at a Sotheby's auction for $25,000.

This divine gift helped to demonstrate the third divine or natural law that what you think about and believe in wholeheartedly is what you get. When you think of wealth, it is delivered. This has happened time and time again for me. Using the same principles and with even greater faith, I went on to sell another painting for close to $50,000.00. (I had never sold a single piece of artwork in my life before.) I was overwhelmed and very grateful for how these divine paintings started to help turn my life around and helped support my family and fund the making of this book during a the time when we were experiencing such instability. Now you know how the Law of Attraction really does work <u>when you let it</u>.

**The Law of Attraction, based on quantum physics, dictates that one's thoughts have an actual physical energy to attract whatever it is the person is thinking of.**

In order to control this energy to one's advantage, you must practice four things:

1) Know exactly what you don't want and what you do want. Then focus <u>only</u> on what you do want.
2) Ask the universe for it.
3) Begin to feel, act, and believe *as if* the object of your desire is already yours (visualization).
4) Be open to receive it, and let go of the attachment to the outcome. (Faith)

So here's the challenge: How do you get your mind to believe that your million-dollar contract is already here?

How do you find the faith that you will succeed in getting what you truly desire in life no matter what?

My conviction, and that of most highly successful people, is that you must simply allow yourself to know deep down inside that *your dream is possible*. You must also understand and appreciate its importance to you as a meaningful goal, as this will greatly increase your desire to achieve it.

As you do this, you will begin to see more vividly how the real value of a dream is not always whether you ultimately accomplish the entire goal or not, but rather who you become and the amazing experiences you have along the way as you are going after this goal.

That, dear friend, is the true secret to how life really works! Life is the ride, not the destination. *Enjoy the ride, and then enjoy where the ride takes you.*

This process works for the individual giving up smoking or the individual wishing to lose weight. You see, if you only knew you were guaranteed to be successful, all of your fantasized fears and apprehensions would quickly vanish.

You would get your unbending strength, energy, and motivation from knowing that if you just keep trying and heading in the direction of your goal, eventually you will get there. You would ask that pretty woman out on a date because even if she said no, you would then know she obviously wasn't the right woman for you, and you would quickly move on from the momentary disappointment because you had absolute faith that the perfect life partner was still out there somewhere waiting for you. You wouldn't sit around crying over the last rejection, because you would be in too big of a hurry to find your true love that you knew was out there waiting for you.

Or, say you just went through a horrible divorce. You might begin to understand how this challenging life transition could actually turn into a new beginning for you. It could instead become an opportunity to find the real true love of your life. If you're willing and able to keep an open mind, even during the most difficult times, you can turn adversities into opportunities!

This isn't always easy to do in the moments when you are struggling, but the payoff is huge when you push through and allow yourself to stretch and grow through the adversity.

The amazing part of this process is you can actually create your own contract with yourself by creating a personal guarantee. In essence, *you have more power and more influence than anyone else* when it comes to whether or not you take action and do all the necessary steps it takes to ultimately reach your dream anyway.

## Make a Firm and Binding Contract with Yourself!

You need just make a firm and binding contract with yourself and keep your "WHY" or dream always in the forefront of your mind. It doesn't matter the size of the dream. It doesn't matter the size of the goal. It can be as small as starting a new hobby like learning to play the guitar or the piano, getting a promotion or salary increase at work, or even losing ten pounds. It can be as big as earning an advanced college degree, improving your marriage, or starting a foundation to help save the lives of people living in less fortunate circumstances than you.

In order to accomplish this, you must keep guiding your thoughts back onto the importance of accomplishing your goal or your "WHY."

You see, the most powerful part of the process is simply staying focused directly on your goal and not letting your mind get distracted with extraneous thoughts or diversions from what's most important in your life! And when you do, *magical things begin to happen in your life*! I've seen it happen time and time again. In fact, this process has worked for me every single time I have used it, and it can for you too.

"Anything the mind can conceive and believe, it can achieve."
-Marcus Aurelius

Perhaps one of the most important and powerful things I have done in the past ten years was to have a vision-bracelet with the words "What's More Important?" engraved on it. I wear it on my wrist constantly to help remind myself throughout the day not to let my thoughts get distracted by other unimportant people, places, or events. It keeps my attention focused like a laser beam aimed in the direction of my ideal future I have visualized for myself, and which I want to share with my family and friends.

The wristband becomes a *compass* that guides me throughout the day and makes once difficult decisions of how to best spend my limited time incredibly easy by grounding me to what's most important.

By simply keeping my thoughts focused on the future I desire, the reticular activating system (RAS) in my brain immediately begins selectively tuning into every relevant thing in the surrounding environment and searching through my vast store of memories, which could be used constructively to get me one step—or a quantum leap—closer to achieving my ultimate goal.

It's like having a team of full-time employees working for me at no cost to make my dreams a reality. In fact, this one single strategy is so powerful, and helped me to transform my life for the better, that I want you to have the opportunity to also benefit from this extraordinary power too.

Go to our website at **SecretToStopSmoking.com** and get a *free* vision-bracelet sent directly to you so you too can begin to experience how it can powerfully propel you toward becoming a non-smoker and at the same time also help you start living the life you really want!

Destiny: The power that predetermines the course of events.

- thefreedictionary.com

Stop! Take this time right now to make a guaranteed contract with yourself. Don't fall into the trap that so many others do of putting off going after their more ideal life. Don't sit around and wait for better circumstance or someone else to believe in your dream. Commit to your dream now and go after it with absolute faith and determination.

When you take this step, you will wake up each day with an amazing fund of energy and passion because you are stretching yourself and having exciting and novel experiences in the process. This energy and passion will propel you—at times even carry you—over any obstacle that gets in your way.

Big dream or small dream, it doesn't matter. We get strength from starting something new and stretching out of our old comfort zone. Only when we are growing are we truly alive. Make your "why" so important that nothing will be able to stop you from doing whatever it takes to make it a reality.

"Courage is not the absence of fear, but rather the judgment that something else is more important than fear."
                                                    - Ambrose Redmoon

Your dream will be an intense magnetic force pulling you constantly toward your goal, on the way it will give you strength you probably never experienced before and will make it exponentially easier to become a non-smoker when you link these two goals together.

Take a second here to have some fun and write down the wildest dream you can imagine. What would you attempt to do if you knew you could not fail? Don't worry about how it will happen, just write it down. (Do you think the very first time Walt Disney thought of building the Magic Kingdom he knew all the details of how it would get done?) Go ahead: have fun and write it down now.

_____

Now that you have your dream clearly visualized, imagine someone has provided you with a guaranteed contract to back this dream. Then write down what would be the first couple of steps you would need to take to start on your way toward accomplishing this goal?

1. _____
2. _____
3. _____
4. _____
5. _____

Now that you have a clear idea of what direction you must head in to eventually get there, why not take action toward this goal and take the first couple of steps? What is the worst thing that could happen if you did? Most likely none of the fears that just raced across your mind would ever occur, but even if one of them did, eventually you would find a way to handle it, and you would survive. In fact, you would most likely become stronger because of it.

"A goal is a dream with a deadline."

- Napoleon Hill

Now here is the amazing part. When you take the first steps, you actually start to become the kind of person who has the capacity to obtain your goal.

You might be wondering what going after your dreams has to do with becoming a nonsmoker. Well, this step is included here because it is an integral part of *The Secret to Stop Smoking*. It will make the transition back to being a non-smoker so much easier when you are also heading toward improving the entire quality of your life. *When you tie the importance of achieving your dream directly to the importance of becoming a nonsmoker, you will experience an increase in desire, commitment, and strength.*

Not doing this is why so many other methods to quit smoking are not as effective. This is because when you combine your goal of becoming a nonsmoker with your goal of living the life you've always desired, you are hitching onto one of the most powerful internal resources human beings possess.

## S T R E T C H... Yourself ... do the thing that makes you uncomfortable... and soon it won't.

The Law of Goal Synergy, which is the term used to describe how two separate goals once forged together create a much greater desire (or internal driving force) than either individual goal could on its own. By combining your goal to return to your natural state of being a nonsmoker with going after one of your most important personal goals, you are exponentially increasing the probability of reaching both of them.

Think about how the young men and women who bravely fought against Hitler's army combined their desire to stop the harming of innocent people's lives and combined it with their desire to protect themselves from facing a similar fate. This ultimately gave them the absolute courage and conviction to face a powerful opponent and eventually be victorious.

This step is so powerful it will help you succeed even during those times when you are facing the toughest of life's challenges. This I guarantee in writing to you!

Go as far as you can see; when you get there you'll be able to see farther

- Thomas Carlyle

A more practical example of goal synergy occurred for Jake, a gentleman who had been in a rather unsatisfying relationship for several years. During that time, he gained a lot of weight and felt insecure about his appearance. He knew the relationship he was in had no real future, but he was fearful to leave it because he feared being alone.

After several conversations with Jake, it was suggested that perhaps if he started to get in shape and lose the weight that made him feel so unattractive, maybe he would start to feel more confident and might even start meeting new people. If he started meeting new people who were more fun, passionate, and attractive than his current girlfriend, and who also really enjoyed spending time with him, he might just begin to feel less in need of staying in such a bad relationship.

By placing his two goals together and working toward both, he quickly and seemingly effortlessly lost 30 pounds in three months. Afterward he was feeling healthier and more self-confident. He was beginning new friendships with other women, and even though he wasn't dating anyone, he no longer felt the need to stay in a bad relationship. He wasn't afraid to leave and live on his own for a while.

The excitement and possibility of having a more loving and satisfying relationship in the near future provided him with the increased desire and passion he needed to help him take the steps necessary to begin losing weight. His desire was so strong that it was almost effortless for him to change his eating habits and begin exercising on a regular basis. This combination of blending his goals together ignited the powerful internal forces, which helped him more easily reach both of his goals.

While it is not absolutely necessary to combine goals, if it makes it easier and gets you double the reward, why not do it!

My personal combined goals are to spend more quality time with my family (which requires being physically, financially, and spiritually healthier) and to help as many people as possible learn the secret to stop smoking and start living the life they really want.

Whenever I become discouraged or overwhelmed, I look at my vision bracelet and think of my most important goals and always find the inner determination to persevere and push forward. You will too, as you begin to implement these time-proven strategies for your own success.

Go for it! What do you really have to lose? Ask yourself how you will feel ten years from now if you never at least tried to reach this goal?

"The journey between who you once were, and who you are now becoming is where the dance of life really takes place." - Barbara De Angelis

When you make a concentrated and consistent effort to guide your thoughts throughout the day back onto your most important goals, you will ultimately be in control of your destiny. **Thoughts are the single most powerful force in our possession, and by concentrating them with laser precision on your goals and then taking action, you are destined to be successful.**

## \*\* Change Your Thoughts, Change Your Future \*\*

# 12

---

# WHO LET THE DOGS OUT?

You may already know the classic behavioral experiment by Ivan Pavlov in which a dog is fed food at the same time a bell is rung. At first the bell only is rung and has no impact on the dog's behavior. However, after several repeated pairings of the bell being rung along with the serving of food, the dog begins to salivate (expect food) when later only the bell is rung. Even with no food present. Thus showing the dog expects to receive the food (relief from hunger) when the ringing of the bell occurs.

For you cat lovers, the same occurs when you begin opening a can of cat food. Just the sound of the can opener is a signal to the cat's brain that a tasty reward is coming, and she comes running.

The same process takes place in the smoker. Through thousands of repetitions, we have come to mistakenly think the cigarette is pleasurable because we anticipate a reward (reduction of nicotine craving). Smoking breaks have become triggers for the anticipation of a reduction of the discomfort of cravings.

So after a while, we imagine we enjoy smoking after a meal, in the car, or with a drink. However, unlike the dog or cat examples mentioned above, we do not receive life-sustaining food as the reward; instead we get a sinister poison that has anything but a healthy, life-sustaining impact on our bodies. Smoking does, however, provide one with an almost immediate rush of nicotine, which in turn stimulates the dopamine pathways in the brain. The major problem with this recurring cycle is twofold.

Black Leaf 40

First, to get the nicotine in the bloodstream, you are inhaling carcinogenic smoke that slowly poisons and destroys the body in the process. In fact, the nicotine itself is a natural pesticide created by Mother Nature to kill off insects that feed on the leaves of the tobacco plant. This naturally occurring pesticide was once commercially marketed under the product name of Black Leaf 40–the forty represents that it was comprised of 40% nicotine. It was an extremely effective and highly lethal pesticide, killing insects feeding on farmers' crops. However, Black Leaf 40's lethality to nearly everything else it came in contact with eventually caused it to be banned from use in the United States agricultural industry. Apparently, nicotine is too dangerous to spray on corn but is fine for humans to inhale.

Second, almost immediately after the nicotine enters your body, it begins to chemically break down and quickly leaves the body, causing a vicious cycle of needing to be replenished over and over to avoid the irritating nicotine cravings. The strong pleasure that one associates with their morning cigarette is really only a reduction in nicotine cravings. This is because during the six to eight hours while one sleeps, the body rapidly breaks down the nicotine levels in the body. This morning craving for nicotine, if simply ignored, would go away on its own.

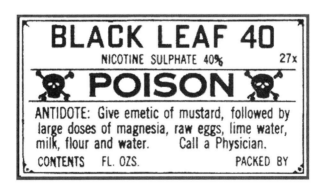

"It's like you were my favorite drug... The only problem was that you was using me in a different way than I was using you... But now that I know that it's not meant to be, you gotta go, I gotta wean myself off of you."

- Rihanna

# 13

## TRUST YOURSELF

This is a quick refresher course in knowing that you were born with an amazing internal guidance system built into your body and mind. The system works like this: we seek that which feels good.

Sigmund Freud felt this was the primal motivator of all human behavior and termed this process the *pleasure principle* because he noted that we are likely to do a behavior again and again when we associate pleasure with it. In contrast, we will move away from or avoid anything that causes us pain or discomfort.

This can also be extended to include our imagination of whether something will cause us pain. Oftentimes it is our imagined belief about what an experience will be like that causes us to actively seek it out or to desperately avoid it.

### Pain versus Pleasure

In a fight, who would win: pleasure or pain? Think about it for a minute. Which do you think is a stronger motivator: feeling good or not feeling bad? Before I tell you the answer, if you don't already know it, there's something extremely important to take into consideration. Not all experiences are purely pleasurable or purely painful. There are often experiences containing degrees of both pleasure and pain.

For instance, when we are very hungry and we have a pizza fresh out of the oven, we want to dive into it. We start to take a big bite, but because of the pain of the hot cheese on the roof of our mouths, we stop eating dead in our tracks. We wait until the pizza starts to cool off a little before our next bite. We may intervene by blowing on it to cool it off, but we are not willing to get burned again, even when we are starving.

All things being equal, ultimately we will attempt to avoid pain before we move in the direction of pleasure, or engaging in a new behavior that will ultimately be good for us. This is why so many people who are always planning to start exercising never even get started. They have come to anticipate more pain with starting to work out than they do with the more delayed good feeling and increased energy that will come later after having exercised on a regular basis.

## Overpowering Perception

Understanding this fifth law is essential to begin to understand why so many people find it so difficult to quit smoking. They have come to anticipate a higher degree of *pain* if they were to stop smoking than they do *pleasure* with no longer smoking. *This basic law of human nature to attempt to avoid "perceived" pain must be overcome before anyone can successfully quit smoking.*

Do not get discouraged. This obstacle is quite easy to overcome when it comes to your quitting smoking. You see, the perceived discomfort created in our minds of not having a cigarette is much greater than the actual physical discomfort that one experiences upon quitting. This is made clear during those times such as on a long plane flight, when watching a movie in a theater that does not permit smoking, or when we go to sleep at night. During these times we don't get overwhelmed with uncomfortable withdrawal symptoms or cravings when we go for hours without a cigarette. It is only when we don't know when we will be able to have our next cigarette that a sense of panic begins to set in.

If you know immediately after the plane lands you will have a cigarette, you are able to manage the flight just fine. But if you start on a flight without a pack of cigarettes on you and are not sure of where or when you can get the next pack of cigarettes after you land, then panic can begin to creep in.

It is the not having the option of having the next cigarette that is a much more powerful negative state than is the amount of time elapsed between smokes. That is why apprehension starts to set in when there are only one or two smokes left in a pack. Ask yourself why this occurs? Why is it not the amount of time elapsed between cigarettes that causes discomfort but more the lack of access to them that creates such intense anxiety in the smoker?

Can it be that the psychological reliance on the thought of a cigarette is actually more important than the actual cigarette? I have seen people go into a full-blown panic over having run out of smokes. Their minds could not be put at ease until after they find a way to get another pack. Why should this be? We don't panic when we run out of bread or juice or chocolate. Of course, we do panic when we run out of oxygen. But clearly cigarettes are not as essential to our lives as oxygen and food, so why do we panic as if they were?

The answer as to why panic sets in has been elusive to many smokers. In fact, many don't even question it any longer. They just make sure that no matter what, they don't ever let it happen. No matter what, they make sure there is always access to cigarettes. This is not that difficult of a task because they have been strategically placed all around us: in grocery stores, drug stores, gas stations, and bars.

# 14

## WHAT YOU THINK ABOUT MOST IS WHAT YOU GET!

Perhaps the reason the steering wheel faces forward in a car seems obvious to all of us now, but there was a moment in time when the person designing the very first car had to decide where exactly to put the steering wheel. Clearly it is easier to drive when you can see what is in front of you. Once in a while, it is also important to know what is behind you, but not nearly as often. But if you stop to think for a moment, the exact same amount of time is spent *driving away* from a particular destination as is the amount of time spent *heading toward* where we eventually want to go. Yet clearly we do not want to look out the back of the car window the whole time as we try to steer toward our ultimate destination.

The same holds true for leaving cigarettes behind you for good.

The reason a majority of the attempts to quit smoking fail is largely because the strategies most people use are designed with the steering wheel facing backward approach.

Let me explain what I mean by this... The focus on quitting smoking and marking off on the calendar how many days since one quit smoking is the typical method used to measure one's progress toward "giving" up smoking. This tends to keep the focus more on what they don't want rather than what they do want.

Do not let this seemingly **small detail** slip by without making a **BIG IMPACT** on you. It's a defining step from having lingering urges to smoke to never having an urge to have a cigarette or a doubt whatsoever that you will never smoke again.

In fact, at times you will wonder how you ever inhaled the noxious smoke without choking and gagging much like everyone does when they attempt to smoke a cigarette for the very first time.

Put another way, the things we think about and desire the most in our minds tend to become our reality outside our minds. If we spend a majority of time thinking of how hard it is keep from smoking again, we will come to find it too hard to quit and eventually we give in.

This is because our conscious mind also has a more powerful subconscious mind working just out of our awareness, which works 24/7 to bring into our lives that which we focus our thoughts on the most. Good or bad, easy or hard, the subconscious mind does not care. It just delivers what you spend most of your time thinking about into your life.

## Switching Direction

This Universal Law of delivering to us exactly what we are thinking holds true for healthy as well as unhealthy thoughts. By simply shifting the focus on concrete ways to improve our health—instead of focusing on quitting—we begin to change what occurs in our lives. Instead of feeling lousy, think of feeling good. Instead of thinking how hard it would be to begin exercising if we haven't engaged in working out in a long time, think instead of how good you will begin to feel as you exercise more and more and get in-shape.

This switch in word choice may seem like a play on semantics, but it is way more than just switching words. It is switching your focus and, therefore, switching the direction of your mental energy toward getting more of want you want rather than what you do not want.

Athletes have long shown this phenomenon on the field or court. One basketball player in a "slump" focuses on how he keeps missing shots and continues to do so. But, the athlete who begins to see how his shots are starting to go in, begins to improve his accuracy and make more shots. The player's skill has not changed as much as his focus has changed.

Focus on the outcome you want and not the one you don't want, and you will get it, and much more. Focus on taking steps toward improving your health by waking up in the morning and doing one thing to begin feeling better right now.

Whether it's taking a walk, jog, or run before you start the day, you will start the day focused on improving your health, energy level, and self-confidence. This positive start will have a ripple effect throughout your day. As you simply start to take these small steps toward being healthier, you will start to feel healthier.

## It All Starts with One Small Step

Even if it's been years since you last exercised, you can always start with a small step. At my lowest point, I probably hadn't exercised for over a decade. I started with building up the energy to take out my jogging shoes. I procrastinated for a month by convincing myself I needed a new pair of running shoes. Then I took another few weeks looking for just the right pair at a cheap price.

Once I got past this resistance within myself, I started the first morning excited but equally knowing I could talk myself out of starting that particular day for any number of "valid" reasons I had running through the back of my mind. As fortune would have it, my house is on a small hill, and it provides a sloping driveway that leads to the street. I simply focused on getting myself to take the first three steps down my driveway, and from there, the momentum of the hill would pull me into my jog. My focus each day after stretching was to simply take three steps down my driveway; from there, another secret of a natural principle reached my awareness. **This secret is that motivation comes *after* you actually start to take active steps toward your goal, not *before!***

## The Biggest Mistake about Motivation

Most people try to get themselves motivated *before* they attempt to do something, which is why most people never get started toward their goal. *If they simply knew that after they started, they would be motivated, their accomplishment rate would skyrocket.* If you don't believe me, give it a try. What do you have to lose?

You will begin to see that while the feeling state of motivation is not something that can always be summoned to the forefront by sheer will, it can be summoned by the act of engaging in a valued activity or goal.

First you must take the action, and then will come motivation.

A funny thing happened on the second or third day I was jogging. While engaging in what I believed was jogging, but objective observers may have called speed walking, I began to hear a sound behind me slowly growing louder and louder. As I looked to see the source of the sound, I saw two much older ladies, probably 25 to 30 years older than I am, running and ready to pass me at a much faster speed. They passed me almost as if I had been standing still, but I had the biggest smile on my face because I was proud to be off my butt and on the road moving at any speed.

I felt pride in my accomplishment rather than defeat in being passed. I focused on the accomplishment rather than my lack of physical condition-ing. Each day I gained some speed and strength, but what became way more important to me as I began to make this exercise routine a natural part of my life was I was gaining a growing sense of energy and focus.

To apply this naturally occurring force to your attempt to stop smoking, you need simply to not wait until you feel motivated to stop, but instead begin to take the small steps outlined in this book to start the process. For instance, if you are a pack-a-day smoker, start to cut down to 15 cigarettes a day instead of 20. Then you cut down to 10 per day instead of 15 a day, and so on. As you do this, you will feel the growing sense of accomplishment and MOTIVATION to reduce the number more and more. Don't overexert yourself by stopping "cold turkey" until you are ready. This is a major trap a large number of people fall into as they have a growing sense of strength in their commitment to quit. Just like exercising too much and too hard at first will leave your muscles over extended and extremely sore the following day so you don't want to exercise again for a long time to avoid the pain, you must also not stop too suddenly. Instead, gradually and consistently reduce your intake until you have successfully gotten the consistency down and the motivation up. You will then have the necessary inner strength to know when the time is right to smoke your very last cigarette.

This phase of slowly reducing your cigarette intake is especially impor-tant because during this time, you are also doing the mental reflections described earlier in the book of looking at how the nicotine illusion works in your body.

This observation time is crucial to allow you to gain the clear perception needed to destroy the illusion. To see nicotine addiction for what it is–an imposture, a fake. To see it for the liar and deceiver it is that never really provided you with good feelings, but simply removed bad feelings in you that it had been secretly creating just outside of your awareness. As you simultaneously do these actions, you will have a growing sense of energy, strength, and accomplishment that will keep you motivated to reach your ultimate goal: becoming a non-smoker again.

"Every thought brings into action certain physical tissue, parts of the brain, nerve, or muscle. This produces an actual physical change in the construction of the tissue. Therefore it is only necessary to have a certain number of thoughts on a given subject in order to bring about a complete change in the physical organization of a man.

"This is the process by which failure is changed to success. Thoughts of courage, power, inspiration, and harmony are substituted for thoughts of failure, despair, lack, limitation, and discord; and as these thoughts, the physical tissue is changed and the individual sees life in a new light. Old things have actually passed away. All things have become new. He is born again, this time born of the spirit. Life has a new meaning for him. He is reconstructed and is filled with joy, confidence, hope, and energy. He sees opportunities for success to which he was heretofore blind. He recognizes possibilities which before had no meaning for him. The thoughts of success with which he has been impregnated are radiated to those around him, and they in turn help him onward and upward; he attracts to him new and successful associates, and this in turn changes his environment; so that by this simple exercise of thought, a man changes not only himself, but his environment, circumstances, and conditions."

- Charles Haanel

# 15

---

# WHAT TOBACCO COMPANIES AND HITLER HAVE IN COMMON

In 1922 the Hitler Youth (*Hitler-Jugend*) was established by Adolf Hitler to recruit and train new members as young as ten years old into his organization. These children would eventually grow up to become the most loyal adult followers of the German Army. This seemingly small and insignificant movement was actually the most calculated and powerful tactic conceived by Hitler to gain power and influence over his entire country and ultimately allowed him to carry out one of the largest mass murders known to mankind. Three years later, in 1925, membership had grown to about 5,000 youths. However, the number of members exploded to well over 8,000,000 by the year 1940.

Hitler's main goal was to take young boys and girls at the stage in their lives when they were most impressionable and systematically mold and manipulate them into faithful followers of his movement. His goal was to indoctrinate them in such a way so they would neither question nor challenge future orders to conduct horrific acts because they had been brainwashed to believe this was the right thing to do by their adult leaders in the Nazi Party.

Propaganda posters were used to conduct and perfect this large scale brainwashing and was unfortunately one of the most successful modern-day advertising campaigns. The ever-present and colorfully designed propaganda posters were used both as a recruiting tool and as a visual reinforcement to existing members of the vast popularity and social approval of the Hitler Youth.

This movement was eventually responsible for the death of over 11 million innocent lives.

## Recruiting Customers for Life

Likewise, the goal of recruiting teenagers and using creative and colorful advertising campaigns to enlist new members and normalize harmful behaviors is used by the tobacco companies. It is no coincidence that nearly nine out of ten adult smokers had their first cigarette before the age of twenty-one, with half of them becoming regular smokers by the age of eighteen, according to the Center for Disease Control (CDC).

The cigarette companies know it is much easier to get teenagers to engage in risky behaviors. Teens are notorious for being curious and willing to try new behaviors while also having a distorted belief of being invincible. The Surgeon General's warnings posted on cigarette packs that declare cigarette smoking as harmful to one's health has little to no impact on them for these very reasons.

Even those teens who mentally register that cigarette smoking will literally take years off their life spans continue to smoke because they don't project that far into the future. It is not an immediate concern to them. For example, one teenager said to me, "Ok, instead of living to 79, I'll die at 75. Big deal." Well, actually the number of years that cigarette smoking shortens the average life span is not four but 14. Nevertheless, this has little impact on the 16 year old to whom it feels like an eternity until he will reaches his 21$^{st}$ birthday.

This is no accident. This is by design. Think back to your very first cigarette. Likely it was when you were a teenager and you tried smoking for entirely different reasons then why you continue to smoke today. Ask yourself if you had never tried smoking before if you would likely go into a store, walk past a pack of cigarettes, and say to yourself, "Hey, I want to buy a pack of these things and see what they're like."

Just doesn't happen. How come? The majority of non-smokers never give a split second thought to taking up smoking. It is as foreign a thought to them as making plans to charter and parachute out of an airplane this weekend. Why is that? If smoking really were doing all the wonderful things attributed to it, such as helping one relax, focus, concentrate, feel less anxious, etc., why wouldn't non-smoking adults at least try it every once in a while?

Because to them, it makes as much sense as inhaling the exhaust coming out of their car after they start it up. This is why the tobacco companies target kids, teens, and young adults. They know the vast majority of individuals who would be willing to "experiment" with this dangerous and addictive drug will not do so after they have matured and lost their sense of being invincible. *And they will have lost a potential life-long customer.*

That is their goal: prey on young kids and get them hooked without them knowing or questioning it, so they become customers for LIFE.

# 16

## MARKETING 101

Buying gas today, I walked up to the cashier, and there was the most colorful and enormous display of cigarettes, cigars, and chewing tobacco. There must have been over 200 different kinds of products—all in shiny cool-looking packages. The display case took up the entire back wall! Hard to miss noticing the neon sign lit up with digital lights displaying the current price of Marlboro regular and menthol smokes.

You probably have heard the old saying about the three most important factors in determining price in real estate: *Location, location, location.*

Well, I have to say the tobacco companies have learned that the same rule applies in tobacco sales. They must pay plenty to the store owners to display their product right at eye level at the checkout counter. Trust me, it's no accident where they are located in the store. It's the same in almost all drug stores, convenience stores, and liquor stores.

But that is not the most disturbing aspect of this marketing as far as I'm concerned. What seems bizarre is that even though cigarettes have now long been established as the number one cause of preventable disease and death on the planet, they are still sold in every country on earth (except one) in their shiny little packages, in well-placed display cases, right in our faces. You won't find any marijuana for sale because it is illegal. You also can't find any cocaine, methamphetamine, ecstasy, or heroin because they are too addictive. Yet the number one most addictive and deadly drug on the planet is right there in plain sight for sale to everyone. In fact, they are cheaper if you purchase an entire carton instead of a single pack.

I never really gave this contradiction much thought before I started to work on this book. This specific fact may not be the one that ultimately tips the scale and helps someone make that final decision to quit for good, but it is worth looking at it as yet another reason it is so very difficult to stop smoking.

## What's Normal?

It is not only in your face constantly; it is also accepted as a normal part of every day life. Please know there is nothing normal about inhaling deadly toxins into your body. If you were to sit in your garage and inhale the deadly fumes from the car exhaust, the police and ambulance would come take you away to a locked inpatient psychiatric hospital because it would be surmised you are suicidal.

But buy two packs of cigarettes at Walgreens drug store and you might just get a third pack for free.

I apologize. I don't mean to be a preacher–like somehow I know something others don't. It's really more my disbelief that my mind somehow allowed itself to be tricked into this whole con game that has been going on for over 150 years. Somehow my mind had sold me out for some false promise of what smoking was doing *for me* rather than looking out and preventing what smoking was doing *to me.* How does one's own mind turn on itself? This is really the question to ask yourself as you continue to smoke:

Knowing cigarettes are slowly poisoning us, why do we continue to smoke anyways?

The answer is nicotine addiction. This is the process that is secretly working out of our awareness and against our best interests.

# 17

## BREAKING THE MAGNETIC PULL OF CIGARETTES

Have you ever put two magnets next to one another and felt them being drawn toward each other? The closer they come to one another, the stronger the magnetic force that pulls them together. There is some invisible force in nature which compels them to gravitate toward each other. This phenomenon is a natural law of attraction.

But take the very same two magnets and reverse one. Immediately they begin to repel one another. These once seemingly inseparable partners now seem to be forced away from one another.

It takes greater and greater force to attempt to bring them next to each other. The closer the opposing poles of the magnets get to one another, the stronger this force pushes them apart. Amazingly, simply reversing the magnetic poles of the two magnets, which seconds earlier were attracted together, causes them to now violently repel one other.

This too is a natural law—an unbreakable and unbendable universal law which occurs anywhere you are all over the world.

Even more fascinating is that this same exact process plays out with the smoker's attraction to cigarettes! Often one feels compelled to smoke almost as if an invisible force were drawing oneself toward a cigarette. But what most people don't know is that by a demagnetization process similar to the one described above, the smoker can become instantaneously repelled by the very same cigarettes he or she was once so strongly drawn toward.

You might be wondering how this works...

First, as long as someone falsely believes cigarettes offer some form of escape from life's stresses or challenges, or as long as one misperceives smoking as only a "bad habit" rather than an addiction to nicotine, and as long as one continues to imbue cigarettes with some kind of magical power to comfort them rather than see them clearly for what they truly do, there will *always* be a strong magnetic pull toward continuing to smoke.

Think about it… how difficult is it to "give up" something you believe is enjoyable?

This process above clearly highlights why so many methods to quit smoking often end in relapse. Time and time again, I have seen this struggle play out. An individual first tries to quit cold turkey using willpower alone. It works for a while, and the person goes on for days and sometimes weeks or months without a smoke. But eventually some life event occurs, which triggers a chain of events that trick the smoker into thinking they need *just one cigarette* to get through the stress.

Soon one smoke turns into two, and then into ten, and then right back into smoking every day again. Next, someone might attempt to use nicotine gum or a nicotine patch or some other new device purporting to help exterminate the cravings. These products may help eliminate some of the nicotine cravings but do absolutely nothing for the much more powerful underlying psychological *false beliefs* that one ever enjoyed smoking or that it was ever relaxing.

## Demagnetizing Yourself

These pills, patches, and gadgets have no ability to lower or erase the magnetic pull of cigarettes and eliminate false thinking, so ultimately the majority of users of these products end up right back as full-time smokers.

Even more regrettable, these individuals become evermore disappointed with the failures of their previous attempts to quit and, coupled with their feelings of intense cravings, they become hesitant to ever make an attempt to quit again in the future. They put off quitting in an attempt to avoid having these negative experiences ever again. This cycle plays out so often it is one of the main reasons so many people claim with the upmost sincerity that quitting smoking is the hardest thing they have ever tried to do.

**This will not be your experience as you begin to slowly demagnetize yourself.**

There is a fast and easy process wherein the strong magnetic pull toward smoking cigarettes you may currently be experiencing can be easily flipped upside down and become a strong repulsion or aversion to smoking. This is in essence a two-step process.

The first step consists of seeing clearly through the deception and trickery that tobacco companies don't want you to ever know about. This will be done rather easily by beginning to notice through repeated observations of just how *nicotine actually creates the uncomfortable feelings inside* you as a result of it being broken down and eliminated from your body. Because this process takes place over a two-hour time period and out of your conscious awareness, the cigarette falsely gets credit for removing these bad feelings.

Smoking replaces the nicotine back in your body almost immediately after you light up, thereby stopping the body's attempt to purge this toxin (natural pesticide) from your body. We will explore this first part in much greater detail in the next chapter.

The *second* and equally important step is to redirect your thoughts when you are under actual stress and anxiety through a variety of techniques covered throughout this entire book. Because when you have an arsenal of healthier and more effective ways to cope with stress, relieve boredom, increase concentration, or relax whenever you desire, you will have absolutely no urge whatsoever to smoke ever again.

When you have a big enough reason for becoming a nonsmoker again, it will take little to no effort to accomplish this goal. The old attraction to this past behavior will no longer have a physiological or emotional magnetic pull over you.

In fact, just the opposite will occur. You will feel completely repelled and repulsed by the thought of ever smoking again. You will begin to look at others still caught in the trap of addiction to cigarettes and feel sorry for them. You will look at their inability to see past the smoke screen offered by the tobacco companies and advertising agencies and see clearly what is really going on.

Now, when you are lying in bed tonight, think of all the benefits of becoming a nonsmoker. Stop and picture what your life will be like using this technique. Stop and ask yourself where you will be in a few years if you don't use these techniques. Begin to get really excited about all the ways your life is going to improve, and say to yourself out loud ten times, "I am so excited I am becoming a nonsmoker."

When you wake up in the morning, you will begin to feel more and more compelled to start thinking differently about smoking. While you are eating a meal, picture how much better your life will be once you've become healthier and gradually lose any of the old urges to smoke that used to surface at those times. Could this be possible?

*Yes.* You can begin to literally de-magnetize yourself by using all the tools described right here!

# 18

## MAGIC TRICK SECRET REVEALED

Ever wonder how a magician is able to have his beautiful assistant lay down in a box on stage in front of a large audience and then proceed to cut her in half with a saw or sharp metal blade? How does he do this without killing her? And how can he then magically put the box and the beautiful girl back together again right in front of everyone's eyes?

As a kid, I kind of knew it couldn't be real because I didn't see any blood. I knew it was impossible, but it sure *seemed* real to me at the time. Even to this day, I am not entirely sure how the trick is done, but I do know one thing: it is definitely *not real*. He is not cutting her in half. It is some kind of optical illusion.

### A Simple Deck of Cards

By chance, I came across a magic deck of cards one day at the dollar store. You've probably seen the card trick where the magician has someone from the audience come up on stage, and he says, "Pick a card, any card from the deck, and don't tell or show me what it is."

Without showing the selected card to the magician, the person then gives the card they selected to the magician to put back in the middle of the deck. The person is then instructed to cut the deck as many times as they like until they are satisfied the cards are completely mixed. And like "magic" the magician picks the exact card they had originally selected. What's more, he does it every single time!

How does this trick work? Could it be that the audience member is actually working along with the magician to pull off the trick?

Well, there are going to be some angry magicians out there when they learn what I am about to reveal... The deck of cards is tapered, or made in such a way that the cards get slightly narrower toward the top end of the card. So when the magician takes the card from the audience member, he then secretly turns it upside down and places it back into the deck. Because the wider bottom side of the card is now the only card facing up with all the other narrower on top cards.

No matter how many times the deck is mixed, it is easily felt out by the magician who then can "magically" pluck it from the other 51 cards in the deck.

*It's really just an illusion*, but tricky enough to fool anyone who doesn't know the magician's secret!

### Nicotine's "Magic"

Nicotine works in much the same way. Within one to two hours of your last smoke, nicotine has almost been completely broken down by your body. This tricky drug has been designed in such a way that the withdraw symptoms created by its absence in the body is experienced by the smoker as an ever so mild feeling of discomfort. It often feels like something is missing or of an emptiness inside us. If a long time elapses between cigarettes, the withdrawal symptoms can create a sensation of irritation, anxiety, and it begins to slightly affect our ability to concentrate.

Once a new cigarette is lit and the smoker inhales the nicotine, the uneasy feelings are almost immediately removed because nicotine is delivered within three seconds to the central nervous system. This system then shuts off the body's attempt to expel the nicotine completely from our bodies, which was our bodies' naturally designed poison-purging mechanism.

Smokers unknowingly attribute this relief from the discomfort they had been experiencing immediately to the cigarette being smoked, and then mistakenly come to interpret the act of smoking a cigarette as "pleasurable" and "relaxing."

**Here again is how the illusion works: Nicotine, once inhaled, almost immediately begins to leave the body. The withdrawal of nicotine from our bloodstream and tissue creates a feeling of anxiety and discomfort in you. Once nicotine tricks you into putting it back**

into your lungs and bloodstream, it then gets the credit for removing these bad feelings–the very negative feelings it secretly created in you to begin with.

If one were to simply wait out this mild discomfort of the withdrawal period for a day or two, the empty anxious feelings would simply disappear on their own. You would quickly return to the state that all non-smokers are always in.

Optical Illusion- Is It Moving?

This is just an optical illusion caused by fatigue. It demonstrates how easily our senses can become vulnerable to misperceptions of reality under certain stressful circumstances. This misperception is similar to our distortion of how we falsely perceive nicotine as somehow making us feel better; when in reality it is only removing a bad feeling it originally created in us!

As you begin to pay closer and closer attention to this process as you smoke over the next few days, you'll begin to see more clearly just how this "magic" trick works. And once you see how the trick is really done, the nicotine trick will no longer be able to fool you. Your ability to perceive this deception will take away the previous advantage it had over you, because you previously didn't know how the trick worked.

As you pay closer attention, you will quickly begin to see exactly how *nicotine is actually creating the bad feelings in you and not taking them away at all.*

This was always an illusion, a distraction of your attention away from what was really taking place.

As you begin to pay more and more attention to uncovering just how the illusion attempts to trick you, it soon becomes the beginning of THE END OF YOUR SMOKING.

What do you see in this picture? Do you see the outline of a woman or man's face? What about a word? Hint…the word is another name for nicotine.

# 19

## THE TRANSFORMATION

You can learn a lot from a four year old—if you are not too distracted by your own thoughts. They have a way about being in the moment, a way of staying absolutely in the present. They know what they want to do right now, and that's pretty much all they care about. They want to do stuff that gets them excited and feels good to them, and they definitely know when they don't want to do something.

Adults, on the other hand, have a terrible habit of keeping their minds distracted by replaying negative past events or anticipating problems they imagine might arise in the future. If we could begin to focus our attention to stay in the present moment, we would begin to experience an awakening to our senses and experience a remarkable transformation—a complete change in one's state, much like the process a caterpillar undergoes as it transforms into a butterfly.

I remember vividly one of the many evenings after work when I was in the backyard with my son when he would follow me around and ask, "Hey dad, will you carry me on your shoulders to the park?" "Yes," I would say. This was followed almost immediately with, "Hey dad, can we to go to the park now?" "Sure, give me just a minute [so I can finish my cigarette], and then we'll go."

Of course immediately after you smoke a cigarette, the last thing you would want to do is put a 40-pound kid on your shoulders and run through the park. My legs would always feel a little weaker and my lungs a little more fatigued afterwards. It took a few minutes to regain my energy and sense of balance.

## What Was I Even Smoking for?

That was one of the questions that used to rattle around in my brain at times like these. Why was I continuing to smoke? What was I really getting from doing this? I knew what I had always told myself—that I believed smoking somehow helped me relax or helped me concentrate. I told myself what every other smoker tells herself when she tries to explain why she is doing something that deep down inside she knows is really hurting her. I created the belief that I *enjoyed* it.

"Dad, can we go now?" "Yeah sure, just give me about five minutes, and we'll definitely go to the park."

I can distinctively remember noticing the sun getting lower and lower in the skyline out toward the direction of the Everglades, which you could almost see from our house. Thinking to myself, there are probably 30 minutes left at most before the sun goes down for the day, but also thinking I had a long day and could use one more cigarette to wind down.

Fortunately, we had a small park directly across the street from us, so we could get there in literally one minute. The proximity of the park and the oversized yard were the reasons my wife and I had bought this particular house we lived in at the time. We had decided without ever seeing the inside of the house that this was where we were going to raise our two young kids. A place where they could be outside exploring and playing and having fun with nature.

"Dad, has it been five minutes yet?"

"Almost, just one more minute, and we'll go to the park."

The sunlight in sky was getting dimmer, and the sun was closer to setting and marking the end of the day. It was getting almost too dark to go to the park now.

"We'll probably have to go to the park tomorrow," I thought to myself.

By this time, my son had already become distracted and left the idea of spending time with me and going to the park way behind on his list of fun things to do. He had moved on to something that fascinated him at that moment, like digging in the sand and filling buckets with water and rocks and then mixing them all together.

While he was playing in the sand, I was in my head worrying about how I was going to get through a list of problems that were swirling around in my mind.

"Might as well have one more cigarette before the mosquitoes come out and we have to go inside for the night," I thought to myself.

Looking around at the house and my son playing in the yard, I caught a glimpse of the irony of the situation. Here I was putting off spending time with my son in order to try to calm down with a cigarette and forget about all the mounting bills and problems related to money. When in reality almost every reason I originally wanted more money and a nice lifestyle was so I could share it with my family.

But here I was with my kid and I was so distant, I might as well have been on another planet; I was certainly not really there with him.

This is where I first started noticing a small sliver of awareness penetrating through my well-formed illusion that I was enjoying smoking because it was helping me relax.

When I was smoking, I did not feel relaxed or connected to myself, let alone anyone else. Anything but relaxed was how I actually felt. I wanted desperately to be less stressed out and find a way to solve some of my mounting financial problems. *I really wanted cigarettes to help me relax.* But it seemed that they weren't powerful enough. Then what on earth was I doing this for?

*Have you ever had a similar experience?*

As the sun continued to set, it cast shadows across the yard (and in my mind). I caught a glimpse of my own silhouette–a man not yet 40 years old bent over a cigarette feeling like a zombie, sleep walking through life. This was how so many days had come to pass over the last couple of years. This was becoming "My Life."

This was not how I imagined I wanted the next 40 years to be... if I would be fortunate enough to have another 40 more years...

## Life: A One-Shot Deal

Suddenly the realization arose in me that there would not be another chance at this particular moment in time. We are all given just one shot to live our lives, and how we choose to spend each moment ultimately determines the quality of the experience we get to have while we are here.

My kids will never be this particular age again. I get to have this time with them–learning to ride a bike and tie their shoes–this one time, and then it's gone forever. Next it will be time for them to learn to drive a car, and then they'll go off to college, and after, maybe get married.

It all happens so fast, and you don't get to go back in time and do it again differently. *That's it.* Once the moment is gone, it is gone forever. It doesn't matter if you have kids, grandkids, or no kids at all. Your life is a one-shot deal so far as we know. What comes after is yet to truly be known.

So perhaps that is what is meant by the few wise people who say that the present is actually *a present*–a Gift from our creator. *What you do with this Gift is up to you.* If you are constantly worrying about the future, or if you are stuck in your head trying to worry about or control what other people are doing or might do in the future, you are missing out of the beauty and peacefulness of the present moment.

If you are attempting to control things and events around you, you lose out on the *present* you were given. What's great about living in the moment–or the Here and Now–is that you get to create with it whatever you want.

"Learn to enjoy every minute of your life. Be happy now. Don't wait for something outside of yourself to make you happy in the future. Think how really precious is the time you have to spend, whether it's at work or with your family. Every minute should be enjoyed and savored." - Earl Nightingale

If you really think about it, there is absolutely nothing that can be done about the past or the even the future. It all happens only in the present. How you want your future to be is always determined by what you do in the present, because it ultimately unfolds to become your future. As the great motivational speaker Les Brown proclaims, "The past is being read, but the future is also being written."

You have the ability to change your future and write a new chapter in the story of your life by what you decide to do with it right now in this moment. It doesn't matter what has happened in your past—even if you have been through the worst circumstances, even if you have had little formal education, money, or family support. All you must know is that *it's possible* to change your future; that future can change only through changing in the present. The decisions we are making each minute.

It was during that evening in my backyard with my kid that I first decided to do a little experiment that ultimately helped shed light on learning the secret and understanding what most everyone who ever successfully escapes nicotine addiction must learn to be truly free.

It is a process that starts from the inside out and not the other way around. You can't take a pill, patch, chew gum, or put a magnet behind your ears and become a non-smoker. You must go through this internal process; otherwise, you are at risk for future relapses or substituting it for other problems. It is simple and easy to do, but it requires a decision to commit to the process outlined here.

## The Scientific Method

The next day, I decided I would put cigarettes through an experimental test—just as I had learned all scientists do when they want to uncover an answer to something they can't figure out. I had learned how to do this back in my research methods course at the University. I would create a Test of my stress and concentration levels before and after each cigarette. It wasn't a formal research study in a lab, but it was a scientific study nonetheless.

You see, I really wanted to enjoy smoking. I really wanted them to be a source of relaxation. In a way, I had a built-in bias toward trying to find a positive outcome in this research study. Well, it was really more of a research *challenge*.

I thought to myself that if I'm giving up time to be with my son, Hunter, at one of the most fascinating periods of his life, when his world is still magical and he still wants to spend time with his dad, then these cigarettes better be doing something for me!

Let me confess something to you here. Deep down, I really felt I needed or relied on smoking. I almost felt a sense of desperation of wanting the cigarettes to somehow be able to magically help me relax and feel better.

This is where one of the most crucial aspects of the secret to stop smoking was revealed for me. Through the process described here, you will have the ability to discover for yourself just how the method works to completely destroy the illusion or trance that most every smoker has been brainwashed to spend their lives in. Helplessly being controlled by urges to feed the addiction to nicotine, and in the process, poison and imprison themselves.

**I began deliberately paying close attention to how I was feeling each moment as I inhaled the smoke. Almost as if I was standing outside of myself watching myself smoking.** With each inhalation during the smoking experiment, I vividly sensed a kind of smoky film enveloping me. It was as if I was walking into a fog that would stick to me.

I clearly began to see then, while the first puff gave a kind of rush sensation, every puff afterward was always a let down. They only made me more tired and lethargic. As I repeatedly focused my attention and observed how I truly felt as I was smoking each cigarette, I soon began to have the illusion of "enjoying" smoking rapidly disappear before my very eyes.

My experience with many former smokers leads me to believe that you will too when you do this experiment yourself.

A funny thing happens the more you pay conscious attention to the process of smoking a cigarette. You begin to see the illusion or *delusion* of smoking for what it really is: a false belief that we have inherited from our culture.

## A Most Important Discovery

As it turns out, there is nothing pleasurable about smoking. Smoking does not magically help us relax or unwind. It doesn't miraculously help us focus and concentrate either. *It has no power at all.* It certainly doesn't help us get through challenging situations in our lives. How could it? It doesn't relieve boredom, and it certainly doesn't make anyone look cool. In fact, it only makes us look more tired and older, smell worse, and feel more ragged and worn out.

As you begin to better understand your own illusions about smoking, the urge to continue to smoke will drop out of your own experience. **It is a clear awareness of the illusion that gives you the POWER to dissolve the illusion, *not intense effort or willpower.*** As you begin to explode the myths others have tried to brainwash us with, you begin to pave the way to transform yourself back into a nonsmoker once again. The natural state you were born in before being fed false messages about smoking when you were young, impressionable, and trusting of others.

Follow these steps as I describe them here and see for yourself how, almost like magic, the urge to smoke begins to disappear. This will not take much time or effort to implement, but it will have the powerful effect of transforming you permanently back into a non-smoker. In fact, once you return to being a non-smoker again, you would rather have someone hit you in the head with a hammer than smoke another cigarette. At least that is how I now feel and how the many others who had become non-smokers again feel about ever being back in the vicious trap of nicotine addiction.

Complete this experiment above, and see for yourself that smoking never really did anything for you, and it never could. It was all simply distorted beliefs about cigarettes.

Perhaps one of the most astonishing realizations for me, and maybe for you as well, is that in the past I had always thought I needed a cigarette to get through a stressful or challenging moment in my life. What I know for certain now is that I had been robbing myself of the credit of eventually being able to successfully deal with all of those challenges on my own by falsely attributing my ability to get through those difficult times to having been able to have a smoke. I wonder if you have done the same as well. All the challenges and stressful moments you have overcome in your life were not because you had stopped to smoke a cigarette during those difficult periods. No, it was despite that you had a cigarette. *You did it on your own.* And in the future, you will continue to overcome any challenge you face without the need to rely on the old, distorted delusion that cigarettes have some kind of magical power to do anything for you.

Trust me, or better yet, *trust yourself.* Do the exercise above the next time you smoke and pay close attention to what is really going on. Each time you do, something will change inside you, and you will begin the transformation.

"I see right through you; I know right through you; I feel right through you; I walk right through you."

- Alanis Morissette

# Part Three

# 20

## It's as Easy as Riding a Bike

I have an important concern I want to share with you before we move on. I strongly suggest you still not hastily attempt to stop smoking just yet. Please wait until you have read the entire book. My concern grows from having witnessed many very motivated and committed people attempt to quit without having a thorough understanding of precisely how nicotine addiction works.

There are several strategies that will greatly assist you as you move toward becoming a non-smoker once again. While you may feel very strong at the moment you first decide to quit, there will undoubtedly be moments when you are not feeling as strong, and a life stressor may trigger you to revert back to this old coping mechanism again. This "slip" would not be that bad in itself as an isolated event, but what often happens is that once there is a slip to having "just one cigarette," most people tend to get discouraged. This leads to a sense of failure. Having the unpleasant experience of failure tends to start a spiraling downward process where it is easy to deceive oneself back into the addiction.

For instance, many individuals I have worked with have said to themselves, "Well, since I had one cigarette already, I might as well just smoke the rest left in the pack." Next thing you know, they are straight back into the nicotine addiction as if they had never escaped.

You see, nicotine addiction is in some ways like riding a bike. Even if you don't ride a bike for a year or even 10 years, once you jump on a bike again and start to move, it's as if you never stopped riding. With a bicycle, you don't have to re-learn how to balance yourself or how to stop without falling down. You just pick up the ability to ride instantaneously as if you had never stopped.

The very same thing happens with nicotine addiction.

That's why it's important to have a plan. First, **the only way to truly ever escape the grips of nicotine is to never have another cigarette again.** Even the "occasional cigarette" that might seem harmless can throw you right back into the addiction. The goal must be to *never* have another cigarette again. We will discuss this concept more in a later chapter, but for now, it is important to keep this as the ultimate goal—never to smoke even one cigarette ever again.

## Learning How

However, please take note that on the way to breaking completely free of the addiction, there will be a learning curve, and there may even be a few setbacks. These are not failures but rather very important learning experiences. For me, the last few cigarettes I ever had were essential for me to learn one of the most important secrets I have gained about nicotine addiction.

One of the very first secrets revealed to me was that cigarettes do not help you become calm or relaxed, and they never did. Second, cigarettes do not help you concentrate or become focused. So use your last few cigarettes as a time to conduct miniature science experiments to see for yourself that smoking does not do anything but remove the sense of discomfort and sense of *dis*ease that it created in you in the first place.

The minute you extinguish your cigarette, the nicotine withdrawal creates those growing feelings in you in a subtle and almost undetectable way. However, as you begin to pay attention and take a much closer look, you will see ever more clearly how this process has been working all along just outside of your awareness. You will slowly but surely begin to have a naturally diminished desire to continue to smoke again. The more you pay attention to this illusion, the faster the urge to smoke again will leave you.

For some, it may still be hard to believe that they will actually not have the urge to smoke. Think about this for a minute. Once you see nicotine clearly for what it is, why would you ever have an urge for something that never provided you anything good to begin with? What would you be missing? The answer is *nothing*. In fact, you will be gaining so much more. You'll gain your freedom back from the never-ending need to continuously feed the nicotine addiction. The incessant withdraw symptoms will leave you forever, and you will regain your health, energy, and vitality, and so much more.

## It's Like Leaving a Bad Relationship... for Good

The best way to describe the feeling of becoming a nonsmoker again is like leaving a bad or abusive relationship. In the beginning, all you can do is think of how much time you spent together and the things you did with your old boyfriend or girlfriend. You might miss the relationship and even feel quite sad. But as time goes on and you meet new people, perhaps even find a new partner, you start to see the old relationship more clearly for what it really was–not so great or you would never have left it.

However, moving on from one's addiction can leave an empty feeling–a vacuum of sorts is created when you no longer engage in this once ever-present behavior. That's why it is tremendously easier to move when you are focused on moving toward one of your important goals and dreams for your life. This focus on the pleasure you will be experiencing in the future will keep you on course. Moving you ever forward without a need to look back over your shoulder of what you have left behind.

Trust me, as you pursue improving the more important areas of your life, *you will forget you ever were a smoker.* Yes, you might even see a person smoking and think, "Why are they doing that to themselves?" Almost forgetting that there was ever even a time when you were ensnared in the nicotine nightmare yourself.

"Until one is committed, there is hesitancy, the chance to draw back, always ineffectiveness. Concerning all acts of initiative (and creation), there is one elementary truth, the ignorance of which kills countless ideas and splendid plans: that the moment one definitely commits oneself, then providence moves too.
"A whole stream of events issues from the decision, raising in one's favor all manner of unforeseen incidents, meetings and material assistance, which no man could have dreamt would have come his way."

- Johann Wolfgang von Goethe

# 21

---

# YOUR BIGGEST FAN!

The Miami Dolphins are my favorite professional football team, and I have been a huge fan since I was a kid. There were many games I went to with my father growing up in Miami where I was fortunate to watch them play with awe and amazement while cheering with the thousands of other fans. As a kid I often fantasized I was a wide receiver on the team. I would pretend to catch a game-winning touchdown pass just as the last second ticked off the play clock, and spike the bay in the end zone to the roar of the crowd.

Last year was a particular low point for the Miami Dolphins as they had gone almost the entire season without winning a single game. They were in position to set a record for having the worst record in the history of the National Football League. Fortunately, they won one game and closed the season with 15 losses, and one very important win.

The very next year, they made a remarkable turnaround, and beyond almost everybody's expectations (perhaps even their own), they won 12 games and lost just five. This was quite an accomplishment as it tied the record for best ever turn around of an NFL team. They secured a playoff spot and received the title of Eastern Conference Champions.

My father and I went to the playoff game along with close to 75,000 other fans. The atmosphere was incredibly intense as you might expect given what they had already accomplished as a team to get into the play-offs. The Air Force even had jets flying overhead, and fireworks were shot into the sky to acknowledge the magnitude of the game. Fans painted their faces in aqua and orange as if going into battle themselves. There was a palpable feeling of energy and excitement before the game even got started.

I share this story not so much to tell the tale of a remarkable team accomplishment but because there is a much more important point that can be gained if we look at another aspect of this sporting event. The point can be best demonstrated by taking a moment to reflect on this question: Why is it such a large number of people feel so comfortable screaming and cheering for the success of a sports team (almost as if their very own life depended on the team winning), but as individuals, we typically won't put as much energy and intensity into cheering for ourselves to accomplish our own goals?

As much as I would like to think that the yelling and screaming I did that day at the game had some sort of impact on making it difficult for the opposing team to hear down on the field below and provided some encouragement to the Dolphin players, I nonetheless had very little direct control over the outcome of the game. The players and the coaches for both teams had much more direct control over the outcome of the game.

This is an important point to take notice of because while we can and will cheer for others to accomplish their goals, we really have only minimal impact on the results of their performance and therefore little impact on whether or not they ultimately reach their goals.

Yet we do have significant influence on controlling whether or not we achieve our own goals. This is mostly because our outcome is directly related to the choices and actions we make toward going after our goal!

### Why Are We Not Our *Own* BIGGEST FANS?

Perhaps it's because we were raised not to be too self-centered or conceited. Or maybe it's because we feel more comfortable believing other people's goals and dreams are more important or obtainable. Or maybe we have tried in the past to reach our goals before and were met with too many obstacles that made our goals seem too far out of reach.

Whatever the reason, it needs to change.

Each one of us has a dream deep inside us we want to accomplish in our lives that is incredibly important, but for whatever reason, we have not taken the necessary steps to achieve them. Perhaps some have taken the first couple of steps toward them but then *temporarily* put them on hold. This is done for many reasons. And it's understandable at times, as we can easily get distracted with a crisis or unforeseen life events. There are many things in life that are also important, but if we allow them to, they can take over our focus throughout our days and the weeks, months and years that follow. These distractions take us off course, and we lose sight of our dreams and desires.

If we don't eventually dare to take the first step toward our goals or stay 100% committed and focused on them, our goals will forever be put off for some later date that may or may not ever come.

So why not become your own BIGGEST FAN today! Make your goal to quit smoking and become healthier and more energetic as important as if your very *life* depended upon achieving it–because in so many ways, it does.

Life will pass by so quickly. We are given only so many days on this planet to enjoy and create something. Don't miss the opportunity of *your* lifetime to have the best and most exciting life possible. See we all have a desire for improving our health, relationships, finances, and spirituality. But we don't make the solid commitment to stay focused on taking all the necessary steps to follow through to ensure they become a reality.

I believe your desire for a better quality of life is as important–in fact, significantly more important–than the outcome of any championship football, baseball, or basketball game, or even who wins *America Idol*. If one of your goals is to improve your health and become a nonsmoker, then you must begin to believe it is the single most important goal on the planet. Why? Because your health is incredibly important. Because you need your body to get around!

When you begin to allow yourself to tune into the real importance of your goal and begin to cheer yourself on with relentless passion toward meeting it, you become more motivated and focused.

If you start cheering yourself on like your own biggest fan, whenever you meet up with obstacles and temporary setbacks, you *will* begin to have the very motivation and strength it takes to overcome them. Especially if you also surround yourself with only those people who are also cheering you on and believe in your ability to succeed.

Stay away from negative people like they have the Plague because their negativity can be just as contagious and harmful to you!

Nothing is more important than you actively *living the life you really want* and deserve and making it a reality. When you begin to make becoming a nonsmoker and improving your health **the single most important goal** at this moment in time and stay completely focused on doing whatever it takes to accomplish it, then it will happen, and it will not be difficult. You see, because you are the only one who has control over your choices and actions, you are therefore guaranteed to be successful!

### You Will Succeed!

You cannot be stopped! There is only one possible outcome, and that is success. Outside factors such as bad weather, accidents, other people's negative behavior, and even world events will have no ability to control the outcome. The outcome is and always will be in your complete control.

You might be wondering how I know this can actually work. You might even be wondering if I can prove this. Well, the best evidence I can provide to back up the veracity of these claims is by the very book in your hands. You see, if you are reading this book, then my long-held commitment and focus on completing it and the steps needed to get it into the hands of people looking to get over their challenge to quit smoking is the best proof I know of that your goal can be achieved if you simply hold your focus and commitment like your life depends upon it.

From the first moment I made the decision to write this book and conduct all the research needed to unearth the material required to explain the process to stop smoking, it took a strong, unbending commitment to get it done. There were many challenges to overcome, but perhaps the biggest challenges were surprisingly the ones I created myself.

I had doubts and fears which would arise to try to get me to give up on my goal. My mind would start trying to find excuses like, "Hey, you've never written a book before. How do you know you can even write?" "If there were such an easy way to quit, then why hasn't someone else found it before?"

But I was able to quiet those fears by telling them to shut up and started talking back to them. I would say, "Hey, maybe I haven't ever written a book before, but I can learn," and I spent months reading books on how to communicate effectively.

## Finding Your "Why"

I also put the focus back on my "Why" (as I call it). The "Why" is simply the core reason your goal is important to you, and it is likely related to the five most important aspects of your life. When you allow yourself to remember this reason, you will be inspired by it, and this will help you get through any challenging times. It will literally pull you toward your dream much like a magnet draws to it another magnet.

My WHY was to find a way for everyone I care about—even those people I haven't even met before—to have an easy, clear, and effective way to become a non-smoker again and enjoy the remarkable transformation that occurs when the fog of the illusion that cigarettes do anything positive lifts for good, and the prison walls of addiction fall and you are set free. This is an amazing feeling I wanted everyone who ever fell into this trap to experience for themselves. If my book could help but one person, then my goal was worth the effort, so I told my fears to shut up and leave me alone.

What is amazing is that when you begin to consistently face your fears, you soon see they are mostly unfounded. The majority of our fears are actually imaginary. They will never come true and only occur inside our own minds. We are constantly paralyzed by the fear of the unknown. But once we confront our doubts, they actually start to vanish, and we see them for what they really are—imagined fantasies.

Just below is the acronym for FEAR used frequently by Zig Ziglar, which you may already know, but it's worth repeating here because it can help you easily remember how most of our fears are unfounded and based on false beliefs created in our own minds.

On the flip side of this same coin is FAITH. You see we are ultimately either chased away from our goal to quit smoking by our false fears or driven and empowered by our faith that we can accomplish our goal. And which force you allow to influence you most determines the eventual outcome of whether or not you achieve your goal (and this goes for any goal you desire).

**F** = False **E** = Evidence **A** = Appearing **R** = Real
versus
**FAITH** = An unquestioning belief without proof, but with an inner sense of knowing it is true.

Once you commit to your goal to quit, the biggest challenge you'll face will be overcoming your own resistance. Almost as soon as a goal is visualized, our minds automatically start coming up with why it can't be done. Some reasons might sound legitimate enough, and unfortunately, if we allow ourselves to falsely believe in them, our dream is doomed before it ever has a chance to see the light of day.

**When there is no enemy within, the enemies outside cannot hurt you**
**- African Proverb**

You must see through this defensive structure for what it is: fear of the unknown. Nothing more, and nothing less. If you simply push past the initial resistance and realize that for as many potential problems that may actually arise to prevent you from reaching your goal, there will be two to three times as many ways to eventually overcome them and make it happen. It may take going over, under, or around the obstacles when they occur, but sure as the sun rises, you will find a way if you want it badly enough. Trust this to be true. If you are committed and want it badly enough, it will happen. There is no other possibility.

Pain and Fear can paralyze us and make us seek something to help numb it, or Our Pain & Fear can motivate & propel us forward to better place; a place where we come out on the other side stronger, wiser, & less vulnerable. In essence, we can use our Pain or our Pain can use us.

As Emerson asserts, "nothing external to you has any power over you." You fear these negative images in your mind simply because you have allowed yourself to believe in them as real, when all the time it is only the mere acceptance of the false beliefs that gives them power and authority. Once you take back your power, they will vanish. That is a promise.

"Fear came and knocked on the door.
Faith answered and found no one there."

- Les Brown

## Fighting Fear

Think about why you haven't stopped smoking before. What are some of the reasons you have given yourself? You will see that most of them are fear of what you are anticipating or imagining might happen. Now that you are regaining your power and ability to conquer the fear, you can more easily move toward your goal. You will soon see that there is absolutely nothing to fear but the fear itself.

In fact, you will come to experience just the opposite of these fears. You will experience the most powerful feelings of elation and joy as you begin to take action toward becoming a non-smoker. **Becoming a non-smoker again is one of the most empowering and freeing experiences you could ever have.** For some, it may sound like an exaggeration, but believe me when I tell you that out of all the accomplishments in my life, nothing comes close to the intensity of the sense of freedom and power I experienced when I finally broke free and made the decision to never smoke again.

When you get to the same point, there will be only positive feelings of strength, clarity, and pleasure. The only negative feelings will be those based on the thought that you will have wished you had not waited so long to quit smoking in the first place.

This has been the most common report I get from people who have used the techniques described in this book. They only wish they had taken action much sooner.

So what are you waiting for? What is the reason you are telling yourself at this very moment why you are not ready to take this step?

Whatever the reason you just thought of, you must come to know that it is only an imagined fear. And that you can quickly dispel and move past any fear by focusing more on the ultimate pleasure you will have once you have quit. Be your own biggest fan and *start consistently holding your focus on your desire to become free and on growing your commitment to improving your life and enjoying a healthier body and mind* that will come from breaking free from the nicotine addiction once and for all.

## The Power of the Written Goal

Here is an extremely valuable principle proven by researchers at Harvard University: they found the mere act of writing down your goals on paper dramatically increases the likelihood of you achieving those goals by 85%. Research has consistently shown that the simple act of writing your goals down activates an internal process that for a variety of reasons has the power to help you maintain your focus and commitment to seeing that goal through to its completion.

In order for the best result, it is important to state your goal succinctly, clearly, and in the positive as if it were already being accomplished. Provide a specific time the goal is to be completed by as this helps increase your subconscious mind's ability to bring your goal to you at an even faster pace than without it. For instance, your goal might be written like this, "I am committed to becoming a nonsmoker for the rest of my life and will have smoked my very final cigarette by the end of reading this book."

So go ahead and take the bold action of writing your goal down to become a non-smoker again right here.

Go ahead and take the few seconds to write your goal, and by doing so add years of health, vitality, longevity, and prosperity to your life.

_____

_____

_____

Signed: _____ (Your name here!)

"Remember that you cannot hope to get results unless you keep but the one idea and do not mix thoughts in your mind. All is yours, but you must take it. The taking is always a mental process; it is believing absolutely. This is divine principle."

Ernest Shurtleff Holmes – *Creative Mind*

# 22

## CLOUD THERAPY

Sometimes the hardest thing in the world to do is to sit still; to not *do* anything. To let your thoughts slow down and your present worries pass out of your mind for just a short period of time; to take a moment to ground yourself. Perhaps this is what some people call meditation.

Try to sit still and listen to the subtle sounds going on around you that you have been unaware of. The humming of the refrigerator, the ticking of the clock, the sounds of traffic and birds far off in the distance that you hadn't really been paying attention to because your thoughts were constantly running and distracting you.

Listen to your own breathing, feel the pressure of your feet on the floor, the smell of the leather on the couch. Our minds can only focus on so much input from the world going on around us, so the majority of the time, we are unaware or disconnected from all that surrounds us.

This process of slowing down and meditating may have been a role that smoking a cigarette had done for us, but with the undesirable effect of simultaneously clouding our vision and putting toxins into our bodies. It was a shortcut, so to speak, for us to take a moment away from everything and disconnect from the constant running commentary going on in our minds—the constant thoughts of all the things we have to do, or should do, or believe others want us to do.

## The Content of Our Thoughts

Really, the majority of the thoughts we focus on have little importance or significance to us if we are honest and aware. Mostly they are things we are preoccupied with but matter very little in the long run.

At first, if you have not taken time to just be still and relax without the distraction of the television, radio, phone, or computer on, it may seem unfamiliar and somewhat uncomfortable. But please take a moment (about ten minutes) to let everything go–to reconnect with your body and senses.

Go somewhere quiet where you will not be disturbed. Take notice of the way you have been unconsciously drawing each single breath into your chest and the releasing of it. Notice your posture and allow your arms, legs, and back to relax.

By taking time to tune in to your senses, you will begin to find that you start naturally letting go of some of the thoughts of things you have been bothered by or preoccupied with thinking or feeling. Taking time to reconnect and regain control over your mind and the directions of your thoughts is an extremely powerful way to dramatically reduce your stress and feel better without needing the old fire stick.

The more you take time to pay attention to removing unwanted distractions and paying more attention to thoughts of things you really value and want in your life (love, success, happiness, romance, wealth), the better you will feel physically, mentally, and spiritually. You don't have to sit with your legs crossed and have candles and incense burning all around you. You just need to permit yourself to focus for a moment and be still. Just *be* with yourself and nature for a brief moment during each day.

One of the quickest and most remarkable ways to get back in touch with nature is to simply pay closer attention to it. For instance, look at the color of the sky just before sunset. In Florida, sunsets can be the most beautiful display of colors melting into one another. The enormous and ever-transforming cloud formations in contrast to the cobalt blue sky at noon can be astonishing if you only stop to take notice.

I have come to call this *cloud therapy*–spending just a few minutes staring at the clouds can allow you to feel relaxed and appreciate more of the amazing beauty in the world that is usually overlooked because our attention is on traffic, bills, or other "problems." Take a moment throughout your day to appreciate the most spectacular elements in nature around you.

It doesn't matter if you are in the mountains, near the ocean, in a park on a lunch break, or just in your own backyard. Take notice of the sky and the clouds and see for yourself. Take a moment throughout your day to just be still. It will be well worth the effort.

"There are two ways to live: you can live as if nothing is a miracle; you can live as if everything is a miracle."

- Albert Einstein

# 23

## WHAT'S MORE IMPORTANT?

Here's another one of the most powerful techniques. It's so powerful that when you begin to use it, you will immediately start to experience a dramatic change. Everyone can, in fact, quit smoking. They do it every day. Each time they have their last cigarette, they quit. If they were to just not put another cigarette in their mouths, the last cigarette they had smoked would have been their very last one forever.

This may sound like a game of sorts, but it's really not, because the key to becoming a nonsmoker again is simply to never start smoking again. After you have made the firm decision and commitment to your goal of becoming a nonsmoker, when your decision is strong enough, the rest will be relatively easy.

The moment when the first thought to have a cigarette comes into your mind, simply take notice of the thought. By actually stepping back and becoming mentally aware of the urge as it begins to arise in you, you can begin to stop the automatic process that in the past typically would unfold. There are automatic motions you go through to get your cigarette lighter or matches. If you were to simply distract yourself long enough, those thoughts and urges would quickly pass. This is done by shifting your concentration to thinking about your commitment to quit smoking, and focus on your bigger goal, such as getting healthier and feeling and looking better or having more energy.

If you guide your thoughts and shift focus for a few seconds on these goals until the urge passes, you will be victorious over the fleeting urge.

We can never completely control our thoughts...but we can "guide" them.... and where we decide to steer them makes all the difference...

### Overcoming Urges

This is the ultimate battleground. The urge becomes a wounded enemy trying to take control of its once-conquered territory, control over your thoughts and mind. Do whatever you must when you are in the heat of the battle. Take these few seconds or minutes whenever you are having an urge and turn your thoughts toward your more important goals of becoming a nonsmoker.

Start talking to yourself if you need to. In fact, I highly encourage you to begin an internal dialogue. Say to yourself, "It's just one cigarette–is this one cigarette worth all my goals and dreams?" "Is this one cigarette worth giving up everything healthy I want in my life?" Nowhere else is it more important to focus your energy and your thoughts and your commitment. Ask yourself, **"What's more important?"** What's more important: to have this one cigarette and give up all my success for this one fleeting moment of what I know will really not be enjoyable and will ultimately start the downward spiral into misery all over again, or simply letting this fleeting urge pass on its own?"

"What's more important" are really just three words, a simple question, but it's so very power if used and will have an immeasurable impact!

As you wear the free bracelet provided at the **SecretToStopSmoking. com** website and implement this process above, each time when a thought to smoke comes into your head, simply look down at the visual reminder of the bracelet, and ask yourself the question, "What's more important?" Is giving into this small and fleeting urge for a single cigarette at this moment really worth giving up everything you've worked for? You see, if you make your goal to become a nonsmoker the most powerful desire in your mind, you're practically guaranteed the ability to push off the occasional urge with the greatest of ease.

### A Clear Answer

When you begin to realize there's something so much more important to you, then nothing in the world, especially a two-minute smoke, would ever be worth giving up your dream. The decision to resist an urge will not be difficult. In fact, it will seem ridiculous to you to even consider giving in to it. This is not a new process, but rather applying something many of us do in other areas of our life.

For instance, people who decide to enter into a committed and exclusive loving relationship do this all the time and wear a ring to remind them of their commitment. They may still have a moment where they might be momentarily attracted to another person, but they simply remind themselves of how important their girlfriend or boyfriend, husband or wife, or soul mate is to them, and the thought of giving into this attraction quickly goes away. They simply ask themselves the question, "What's more important, meeting someone new, or having the most valuable relationship in their life be based on trust, respect, and commitment."

To *decide what's more important* is a no brainer when you have a good relationship. Leaving that person or cheating on him or her would seem insane because it could cost the most important thing in your life. A fleeting urge or attraction will have little power to influence you because you've compared it to something so much more powerful.

The same process holds true with smoking. Now that you realize you've never really gained anything from smoking, and that each time you have given in and fallen back into the smoking trap, you lost your freedom, health, and sense of self-control, you know giving in again will only start the merry-go-round of addiction all over again.

You now can see that "one cigarette" can throw you full-force back into the vicious grips of the addiction as if you never left, and that is the last thing you would ever want!

It's really not "just one cigarette" you're choosing to smoke from now on. It is choosing to fall back into the addiction. Once this concept has crystallized in your mind, the lie of "it's just one cigarette" will never fool you again. That's a promise!

This is the place where most people who don't fully grasp the concept fall headfirst back into the addiction. Not allowing yourself to ever have just one cigarette again may sound quite simple. It sounds rather obvious and not a thing of monumental importance; however, it is *essential* to grasp mentally and implement for life.

In your mind, do this experiment: Ask yourself each time before you decide to give in to a fleeting urge to smoke a cigarette, "What's more important?" The answer will come to you each time you do this. Over and over again as you ask the question with each cigarette, the answer will become clearer and clearer 'til you won't even need to ask a question anymore.

"The key to success is to focus our conscious mind on things we desire, not things we fear."

- Brian Tracy

# 24

## TOO SMART FOR YOUR OWN GOOD

Today I woke up and found an article in *People* magazine on the recent passing of one of the top-selling authors of all time, Michael Crichton. Attempting to write my very first book, the article caught my attention. In it I found he was a Harvard Medical School Graduate who had sold over 150 million books and won an Emmy award for the creation of the hit TV show *ER*. Ten of his books were made into films; the most famous of them, *Jurassic Park,* grossed nearly one billion dollars. There was one sentence at the end of the article that mentioned he had died an untimely death at the early age of 66 due to throat cancer.

Sixty-six years old? That struck me as odd for some reason. Throat cancer. Is that curable? My mind went right to where it always does these days… I wondered if he had been a smoker. It wasn't mentioned in the article, but with a quick Google search, I was able to confirm my suspicion as, in fact, true. Michael Crichton, an obviously brilliant and talented man, had the same Achilles heel as so many of us. With all of his passion and brilliance, he too was addicted to nicotine in cigarettes just like one out of every three men on the planet.

### Scare Tactics Never Work

I made a promise at the outset of the book not to use scare tactics or fear at all in the book. Not so much as an attempt to be a purveyor of all that is good and positive in the world, but because I knew perhaps better than most that scare tactics just don't work. They certainly never worked on me! I had researched all the ads online and videos on YouTube that were meant to scare the hell out of all smokers in an attempt to get them to stop poisoning themselves, but underneath every video were thousands of comments by young and old stating the video they just watched of someone's lung as black as coal and lying dead from smoking on an autopsy table just made them want to go outside and smoke even more than before they had watched the video.

The scare tactics actually had the exact opposite effect than the intent! Why is this? We'll get to the answer to that in a minute, but I want to take a second to tell how I came to this realization some time before by a more personal account.

Both of my grandmothers died from complications related to their lifetime smoking "habit." I had myself grown up watching them smoke and spend the later years of life coughing the dreaded smokers' cough. I'm sure you recognize the smokers' cough: when you hear someone trying to clear her throat, but no matter how hard she tries, she just can't get it cleared. As there is no resolution to the discomfort, the body simply adjusts to the state of feeling permanently in a state of *dis*-ease. Perhaps the more shocking aspect was that my Granny had cancer of the mouth, and at some point in her life, I believe it was when I was about 20, she had a large portion of her lower jaw surgically removed to cut out the cancer that had embedded itself in her jaw. She was left permanently disfigured and had to eat only soft food for the remainder of her life.

Anyways, her predicament in particular stood out to me as her daughter, my aunt, was also an avid smoker. I loved my aunt dearly as she is one of the most caring and loving individuals I know. But what struck me as odd is how after having watched her own mother have almost half of her mouth surgical removed she could continue to smoke, or that *I* could continue to smoke. How were we able to continue to engage in a behavior we had seen firsthand cause such destruction? It was to be a mystery that swirled around in the back of my mind for decades.

## That Will Never Happen to Me

It wasn't until much later I was able to figure out the riddle of how so many smokers can watch those around them suffer the pain and indignity of the physical fallout of medical problems directly related to smoking and continue smoking themselves.

It is the very fact of how long it takes for the poisons to do their damage in the body that allow the smoker to look at others and say to himself, "That will never happen to me." You see, every smoker believes he will long have left the nasty "habit" of smoking behind way before it can take its destructive toll. The good news here is that if they were to quit now, that would likely be the case. As within a relatively short period of time, the majority of the damage caused to the body can in fact be mostly reversed.

The body has an amazing ability to heal itself and recover to its original state. The best example of this ability to heal on the inside can be seen by our bodies' ability to heal itself on the outside. Think of the last time you had a small cut or scratch on your arm or leg. At first there may have been some blood or minor pain, and you may have put on a bandage to stop the bleeding. Eventually the wound formed a small scab and the scab grew increasingly smaller and then fell off. The skin below the bandage was renewed and you probably could never even tell you had a cut on that area of your body later on. Your body simply manufactured new skin where the old skin was damaged. Scientists tell us that the entire human body is in a constant state of rebuilding and repair, so much so that you basically have completely new cell bodies every 11 months.

## The Real Problem

The real problem with this process of self-deception is how the smoker does not take into account precisely how cigarettes are purposely manipulated and designed with higher levels of nicotine by the tobacco companies in an attempt to keep them as a *customer for life*. There single main goal is to keep you a life-long prisoner addicted to their highly profitable product.

The common smokers' theory is ultimately flawed in that it presumes that "some day" in the near future they will eventually just get tired of smoking and simply move on from the dirty and nasty little "habit" of theirs. But what statistics clearly show is that day never comes. The "habit" or, more accurately, addiction is cleverly and wickedly designed to lull you into a false sense of security that you could easily quit if you want, while also attempting to hide the harmful side effects of its dangerous carcinogens which enter your body each time you inhale to get the tiny dose of nicotine.

The other insight here that has emerged for me, and will for you, is that the very nature of the long period of time it takes for the carcinogens to show any major effects to our bodies is part of the cigarettes' sneaky ability to trick us into not being worried. It's not like right after we have a cigarette we start coughing up blood. When a young smoker hears someone tell them, "Hey you, better quit before you get lung cancer," the smoker laughs to himself and says, "I'll be long done smoking before that ever happens to me." And they really believe this to be true.

What they are unaware of is how the days of smoking turn into months, then years, and then decades. After a while, we quit even noticing the slow deterioration of our bodies because we think to ourselves, "Oh I'm just getting older, and my body is naturally aging. These bags under my eyes and my aged skin are not from my smoking."

This ability to not perceive the slow nature of the negative consequences caused by smoking is one of the major reasons cigarette smoking continues to be the number one cause of preventable disease and death on the planet.

## Smokers Are <u>Not</u> Stupid

Anyway, I will try to stay true to my promise of not becoming too morbid. Mostly because I know it only creates internal anxiety, which makes one want to smoke even more. That is until one fully learns *The Secret*. What is important to take away from these observations is that smokers are not stupid. In fact, it's quite the opposite. Like the Harvard Medical School Graduate and Best-Selling Author Michael Crichton, most smokers are extremely bright and successful. I believe it is because of our high degree of intelligence that we are able to use highly structured defense mechanisms to falsely minimize the dangers of our own smoking; thus permitting us to continue to feed our addiction to nicotine and fuel the even more addictive and self-destructive psychological dependence on our dirty little, well, "addiction."

So the good news here is you are probably very intelligent. The bad news is that your addiction uses your intelligence against you to hide the subtle but growing negative side effects of smoking from your conscious awareness. Fret not, because the secrets revealed in the following chapters will slowly remove the cigarettes' power of deception and will ultimately allow you to break free so your body can quickly restore itself through its own natural healing power back to the healthy state it strives to be in. These restorative powers will bring about an increase in energy and alertness and even a greater appreciation of life. The application of the principles of *The Secret* will permit a cleansing of our senses, so we appreciate more fully all of the smells and beauty of everything around us.

As you read on and learn the final steps of how *The Secret* works, you will begin noticing a change in yourself. You will be rewarded with a return to a more natural and powerful state of your body, mind, and spirit. So we need not be ashamed of our past inability to see our addictions clearly. We can learn now to do what unfortunately many of the other bright and talented individuals before us never learned to do. We can learn to quit way before it is too late.

A sad addition to this chapter is that as I was about to finish writing this book, Patrick Swayze, the dancer turned actor who was popularly known for his physical grace and great looks in films like *Dirty Dancing* and *Ghost* died at the age of 57. He stated in an interview with Barbara Walters that he believed his decades of smoking had contributed to his cancer. His smoking was a battle he was not able to conquer, as he continued to be seen smoking until his final days.

# 25

## Hurricane Warning

What may have just happened is that you read the previous chapter and might even have allowed yourself to believe most all of it was true. However, if you are like most every other smoker I have met, myself included, you soon started to let that little voice in your head start telling you that even though this may be true for Michael Crichton and Patrick Swayze, you are different.

Somehow, you will be one of the individuals who can escape unharmed by a lifetime of smoking. It would be best to question this form of logic right now. Take a minute to consider this: while this could be possible, the odds are against all of us that we will be unaffected physically. Cigarette smoking is a slow and insidious tyrant who first enslaves us to feed a constant supply of nicotine to our bodies to avoid withdrawal pangs while it slowly destroys our bodies in the process. Then it discards us and moves on to other young victims.

What's most sinister about this is how it can hide all the harmful effects it causes on the inside. There is a slow but steady damage being done, and *the very nature of just how slowly it breaks the body down is its greatest weapon to fool smokers*. Because the effects are slow, small, and steady, we can dismiss each new negative consequence. When we get another cold, or when we start to see our teeth getting stained, or each morning it's tougher and tougher to get out of bed, we are able to dismiss the warning signs.

But know this, there is a steady process going on just under the surface, and it is sending you signals. The most important question is, *when will you act on the warning signals?*

## Early Warning Systems

Living in Florida, there is a yearly occurrence which has become a part of our routine way of life. Each summer marks the beginning of hurricane season. There is a constant reminder by the National Hurricane Center each time a storm system forms out in the Atlantic Ocean. While most of these storms never grow any larger than a tropical depression, some form into full-blown hurricanes. The level of strength and intensity of these storms are categorized, with a category one storm being the smallest and a category five storm being the most ferocious and deadly of all hurricanes.

Recently there was a steady line of several small hurricanes battering our shorelines. At one point we were even hit by the very same hurricane twice in one week as it hit the coast and then literally made a U-turn across the peninsula and struck Florida again.

The steady flow of small hurricanes caused only moderate damage to some people's homes and knocked out power for a short period of time. While this was rather inconvenient, most people simply adjusted and got used to this unusually high volume of hurricanes coming ashore during this particular year. This complacency was to become a costly mistake for some.

After one small hurricane named Katrina hit the Florida coast, it quickly shot across one of the smaller parts of the peninsula and went out into the Gulf of Mexico where it found exceptionally warm waters to fuel its rapid growth. Within two days, it shot from a category one to a category five hurricane. It probably could have been a six if the scale had gone that high. It was aimed straight for the city of New Orleans. The National Hurricane Center began issuing severe warnings to everyone in that low-lying region to immediately evacuate out of the storms trajectory.

I remember this vividly as my father was born and raised in New Orleans and we had lots of family still living there. At this time, many of our relatives began the two-day exodus driving out of New Orleans in bumper-to-bumper traffic and came to stay at our homes in South Florida. There were others, however, who had seen many of the previous storms do little damage. Or had lived through many hurricanes in the past, so they were lulled into a false sense of security, thinking this storm would lose its strength before reaching land as so many hurricanes do. Or thinking they could ride out the storm by securing their windows and doors with plywood and storm shutters as others had done before. Regrettably, some people were so old and sick or lacked the means of transportation and were unable to leave their homes before the storm reached land.

Just like with the two hurricanes that had struck earlier this year, Katrina had lost strength and was reduced to a Category 3 hurricane just before it reached the city of New Orleans. While Katrina damaged some property quite badly, most people were not injured and felt they had been spared a far worse fate had it made landfall with its original strength and fury at its peak wind speeds of 175 miles per hour. In fact, many people felt very fortunate, and even the national rescue teams that were expecting a major catastrophe were lulled into a false sense of security after having seemingly avoided a nightmare of death and destruction that a Category 5 hurricane could have brought had it reached the city of New Orleans. Work to restore power and provide food and water to citizens began as usual. That night after the storm, people went to sleep feeling a sense of relief and comfort, believing they had escaped a potential disaster.

## A False Sense of Security

What they didn't know is that as they slept that night, a system of levees designed to hold the water back failed, and the water from the storm surge began pouring into the lowest levels of the city. In the middle of the night, people woke from their sleep in alarm and in a state of understandable panic. They began trying to go upstairs or into their attics to avoid the rising water levels. Some people even went on the roofs of their homes. Many were trapped in their homes as the waters continued to rise, and tragically, they drowned. Regrettably, the false sense of security felt by most everyone became a deadly trap that ensnared thousands of innocent people who perished in this deadly storm.

The same type of warning is being sounded off this very minute. As you continue to smoke with a false sense of security that the harmful effects of *just one more cigarette* will not cause you any permanent harm, you're being fooled. When will you stop kidding yourself into thinking you are not addicted and will quit before anything permanent happens to you? This is the sinister trap that the tobacco companies "bank" on to continue to profit from your addiction to nicotine.

Heed the warning signs and make plans for your escape before, as with those in New Orleans, it is too late. Ask yourself why, if you could quit so easily, you have not quit already?

## Remember Gary?

Now is a good time to go back to the gentleman named Gary I mentioned earlier in the book who had quit smoking but gained some weight. Well, Gary let me in on why he had so quickly been able to quit smoking after being a pack-a-day smoker for decades. You see, he had found out he had emphysema, a progressive and irreversible lung disorder, from his medical doctor. This condition does not go away once it reaches a certain level. It only gets progressively worse. The best one can hope for is if they quit smoking immediately that it will slow the disease process. Gary's original plan, like so many others, was to continue to smoke up until it started causing more serious health problems. He told himself as soon as that time occurred, he would quit and walk away for good. Unfortunately, like so many others, that is not how the plan worked out. Instead, he quit after it was too late.

He asked that I share his story with you because he wishes that no one else ever go through what he now is experiencing. You see, what happens to most people is they naively go through their younger lives being able to ignore the small warning signs that smoking is taking a toll on their bodies in hopes they will one day have a moment of clarity and just quit smoking. They know if they were to stop, in most likelihood, their bodies would be able to fully recover.

What they don't plan on is that their addiction is the one really in control and that day will never come *unless* they take over control and make the conscious decision to become a nonsmoker now, while their bodies can still recover.

## Planning Your Escape Route

Be one of the survivors who were able to heed the warning signs and plan your escape route now. Do not put this off any longer. The time to escape is not when the storm arrives. *The only way to avoid the catastrophe is to escape before the storm ever reaches you.*

My mission is simply to be able to get more people to do what they already really want to do but keep putting off for sometime in the future. All those I speak to know in the backs of their minds that smoking is slowly damaging them, and they want to quit, they really do, they just aren't ready to do it today. Know this: if you wait for that perfect day to come when you are "ready," you will be waiting forever.

**Quitting smoking is really quite easy. It's making the decision to do it that people struggle with.**

If they only knew what was on the other side is so much more rewarding—a lifetime of renewed health and youthfulness. You aren't losing or giving up anything. It is just the opposite: *you are gaining everything!* The only thing you are really giving up is the inevitable consequences from continuing to smoke: growing health problems, premature aging, bad breath, and fatigue that comes from getting your next fix to keep feeding the nicotine addiction. If you allow yourself to truly come to understand this, then the decision will be easy; in fact, you will not have much to do.

After you make the final decision to become a non-smoker, you need just make the firm and unbending commitment that no matter what, **you never again have a single cigarette or tobacco product**. And this will *not* be difficult. You will see that after some time, starting again would be the last thing you would ever want to do.

### Dive in and Do It!

I know you are going to be successful. There is by now, if you have made it this far, a crystal clear realization of what you are going to do. The thing is to just take the dive and do it. You will be so glad you did. After you have made it through and are on the other side, I would ask that you simply share with others what you have read and learned here and how remarkable and easy the process was. Had you not taken the plunge yourself, you would never have imagined how simple and easy it really was all along.

Please encourage others to read this and go through the very same process described here. If more people learn the secret to stop smoking and start living the lives they really want, it would be the greatest reward I could think of and would have made all the effort worth it.

# 26

---

# THE BIGGEST OBSTACLE TO OVERCOME

It sounds reasonable enough to us when a little voice inside our heads says, "I am going to do it, but I just want to wait until I get past this one difficult thing in my life right now." The one thing for you could be a bad relationship, a major project at work, a financial crunch, or something else. There can be as many reasons to wait as we allow our minds to create for us. Some of the reasons will have very good justifications and will be very attractive to give in to. This is the fruit of the poisoned apple, so to speak. Once you allow anything outside of you to be the source of your timetable for quitting, you have lost the battle.

This is why waiting for your best friend or your husband to quit with you can be the kiss of death to your escape. It sounds like a very logical method. Quit with a partner you trust who will hold you accountable to your commitment to quit—a person who will be there to encourage you when you are having a particularly difficult day. Trust me, this is a trap.

There is only one person who can help you move on permanently, and that is **you**.

This is not to say you should not look for support from other people. Having others to encourage you is a powerful asset. This is why we have a support group online for everyone who wishes to hear what others have done to move on from smoking for good. There is no charge for the support group, and it can be easily found by linking to it from our website SecretToStopSmoking.com. But know up front that ultimately you will be your biggest ally on this journey. Your own fears and doubts will be your own biggest obstacles to overcome as well. Let me explain what I mean by this...

## False Promises of Tomorrow...

Many people have a lingering hesitation inside of them that tells them right now is just not the right time to make the commitment. Our minds are created in such a way that if we allow them to, they will come up with very good reasons for putting off doing something important. This is just how our minds work.

There will be a time when you sit back and out of the blue an idea comes to you that it somehow just will be easier to make the firm commitment to stop smoking a little later on, like after you get through this very stressful new project at work, or after the kids are in school, or move out and go to college.

All of these reasons will sound logical and legitimate at the time. They will be most tempting to believe and give in to.

Do not buy into their false promises of an easier tomorrow, because it will never happen! It will always become, "Well, today isn't so good," or "No, not today, I'll start tomorrow."

## There Is No Better Time than Right Now

It is only by contending with challenges that seem to be beyond your strength to handle in the moment that you can stretch and grow. Start planning your break, and then take the plunge and never look back. Perhaps the single biggest factor that separates successful people from non-successful people is their willingness and ability to make a decision and then take action on that decision. They keep their commitment long after the positive feelings of the moment have left, and they remain committed even during the difficult times when they don't really feel strong and want to give in.

In fact, these moments of low motivation are what lead to having renewed commitment in the long run because they build a feeling of strength and satisfaction that only comes from sticking to your promise to yourself.

"Success is the sum of small efforts, repeated day in and day out..."
- Robert Collier

How will you know the right time to make the final decision and commitment to quit smoking for good? That is a very good question and one you can easily find the answer to with a little introspection. A quick way to make an assessment is to ask yourself this question right now: knowing everything you now know about smoking, considering how many years you have been smoking, if you could go back in time to before you had your very first cigarette, would you still decide to go ahead and start smoking all over again?

If the answer is NO, then I suggest you keep reading. If the answer is anything other than no, it might be wise to stop and go back and re-read the previous chapters.

No one I have asked this question to who has given it significant thought has ever said they would go back and start it all over again. Once it becomes crystal clear you wish you had never made the decision to start smoking in the first place, then it now really only makes sense to immediately stop putting any more of your valuable time, energy, and good health into the addiction.

While you can't go back and undo the past, you can change the present.

"There is a divine messenger detailed at every birth to follow the individual through life. This divine messenger acts as guide, is always pointing out the right road and cautioning against the wrong. If we follow the divine promptings, we shall come to our own."

- Orison Swett Marden

You will know what is best for you by simply paying closer attention to your true thoughts and feelings about what you want for your future. Knowing each decision you make today dramatically impacts the rest of your life. The more you allow yourself to be aware of this, the more you will begin making dramatic changes in your life. Joe Vitale, in his book the *Attractor Factor*, provides clear guidance on how this process works. **The** simple act of focusing your attention away from what you DON'T WANT in your life and instead focusing on what you DO WANT in your life starts the process of bringing more of what you want and less of what you do not want.

Again, this sounds simple, but it's not always easy to do. Is it worth it? Absolutely!

**The Axiom of 3's**

This focus cannot be just once in a while; it must be a constant and sustained focus. Most true change will take a concerted effort, usually a minimum of three weeks. This is the length of time scientists have found it typically takes for something to become fixed in our lives as a pattern. Here is what I call the **Axiom of 3's**: While we already know it takes *3 seconds* for nicotine to register in our brain receptors after lighting up, it takes a considerably longer time for it to completely leave our bodies and for the long-engrained habit to be completely removed. When you immediately quit smoking, it will take just *3 days* for all the nicotine and cravings to completely leave your body. During this time, it will help to drink plenty of juice as it will help your body with its adjustment phase.

Also it is important to give yourself rewards for each goal you accomplish. Rewarding success makes you want and desire more successes and has a positive spiral effect. Next, it will take maintaining a relatively steady vigil for the following *3 weeks* to ensure you keep your focus on maintaining your break from the addiction. The final *3 months* require just sporadic reminders to yourself of the benefits of your newfound freedom and renewed health. These occasional reminders should reinvigorate you and help maintain your commitment to being a non-smoker. Wear the free vision-bracelet during the entire 3-month period to help remain focused on your goal and help ensure your success.

# 27

---

# FREE AT LAST, FREE AT LAST!

So here is how the story, but not the journey, ends. Eventually my family's home–the one with the beautiful yard across from the park–fell into the first stage of foreclosure. It was very difficult for my wife and I to explain to our children how they might have to suddenly leave their bedrooms they had decorated all by themselves and leave behind their large decorative playhouse we had built together in the backyard. But taking everything into consideration, it was after all just a house.

It struck me afterward that our bodies are the "house" we all live in. Eventually, we will all one day be evicted from that house too. The difference is the house my family and I lived in for those many years could easily be replaced if necessary. We could easily move into a smaller home or rent an apartment. But unlike the brick and mortar homes we all live in, we cannot buy another body.

## One Body for *Life*

We get just one body for *life*. There is no trading it in for another one. What I learned during this difficult transition in my life was that losing a million dollars was not really such a bad experience because I had learned a much more valuable lesson from it. And in the process, I found the secret to leave behind smoking forever.

I came to an understanding that if I had continued to battle the world of stress head on by trying to control everyone and everything around me, and had I continued smoking cigarettes, even if I had eventually earned 10 million dollars, it would have been useless to me later on to restore my health or get back the years I spent being stressed out and disconnected from my family. Perhaps the greatest reward was that my wife also learned *The Secret to Stop Smoking* and no longer is stuck in the deadly trap of nicotine addiction.

You see, all the money in the world becomes worthless to the one in two smokers who eventually die from cancer caused by their smoking. It is literally a game of Russian roulette where you never know when the next cigarette will be like pulling the trigger.

## Gaining Greater Value

Here is one of the final secrets to stop smoking. It is a simple yet powerful law. **This law mandates that you can only ever truly leave smoking behind when you finally realize you are trading it in for something *much more valuable*.** Fortunately, this is really the easiest part of the process.

Now that you see that all of the reasons you could ever possibly want to smoke are so small in comparison to the enormous gains of improved self-confidence, physical health, and ultimate pleasure in life that comes from the return back to your natural state of being a non-smoker, you now realize it is an easy transition to make. It just took you being able to see clearly through the smoke screen and brain washing created by the industry that profits off the selling of death and disease to millions. As the smoke screen clears, you are able to release yourself from the self-imposed prison and walk straight out of the nicotine trap forever.

# 28

## THE BEST WAY TO PREDICT THE FUTURE

This last step is the most crucial aspect of *The Secret to Stop Smoking*.

Everything that has come before in essence was to prepare you to be able to recognize the power you have always carried inside you but were not aware of because up until now your powers laid mostly dormant deep inside you. Much like with a loaded gun, it is only the *act* of pulling the trigger that releases the gun's awesome power; up until then, a gun is really just a piece of heavy metal.

When you make the firm and absolute decision to never smoke another cigarette again for the rest of your life, and commit that there will never be an exception, it is like pulling the trigger of a loaded gun and killing any urge to ever smoke again. An internal explosion will occur that changes everything. You will not hear the explosive sound like when firing a gun; instead something will simply click inside you, and the internal battle will have ended.

You will go to sleep and as you wake the next morning, you will know you will never smoke again, and you will feel free. That is the power of finally making a true decision—never to allow yourself to even question that decision.

This decision becomes an internal standard set in stone. It is similar to the way most people know deep inside that they would never murder another person. There may be many challenges and adversities and impulses of intense anger in our lives, but we never question our internal decision that we will not kill another person. There is no debate. It is this same internal certainty that emerges once you finally commit to this act of decision. It is over and done with.

Howard Thurman best describes the power of true decision in this way:

"It is a wondrous thing that a decision to act releases energy in the personality. For days on end, a person may drift along without much energy, having no particular sense of direction and having no will to change. Then something happens to alter the pattern. It may be something very simple and inconsequential in itself, but it stabs awake, it alarms, it disturbs. In a flash, one gets a vivid picture of one's self–and it passes. The result is a decision. Sharp, definitive decision. In the wake of the decision, yes, even as a part of the decision itself, energy is released. The act of decision sweeps all before it and the life of the individual may be changed forever."

### True Freedom

This is the last step and final step of the journey. I must tell you that the most exciting part is really just about to occur. I can vividly recall as if it were yesterday when I made the decision clear in my mind for the first time. What I couldn't have possibly known at the time was the magnitude of how that single act of deciding would change everything.

It took time to understand how that single act removed all the desire and urges that had always followed every other one of my many failed attempts to quit smoking before. How prior to this time there was always doubt and uncertainty– still a struggle to *try* not to smoke. **This act of decision ends the struggle and releases you. This final step allows you to become clear in your mind and you are set free**.

I wish you success on your way toward taking this final step. It is hard to accurately put into words the amazing changes that are in store for you. It will be as if an enormous weight has been lifted and the chains removed. I look forward to seeing you on the other side.

Hold this image of your desired future in your mind, and let it guide you as you go on to make your ultimate decision; *knowing whether you decide to quit or not, either way you are making a decision*. You have the power in you to decide because you know you are not really "giving up" anything, in fact it's the exact opposite, you are "gaining" everything by moving on.

Make a decision to change; then take action on that decision and never look back!

I wish you much success and happiness as you make the final decision. You truly deserve to be happy, healthy, and prosperous in every way. As you make the decision, you will soon see there really was never anything to fear or miss. It was all just an illusion. And you will see for yourself just how amazing it is to be on the other side of the wall. To be free forever!

"To guarantee success, act as if it were impossible to fail."
                                    - Dorothea Brande (1893 – 1948)

"To let it go, and so to fade away. To let it go, and so fade away
I'm wide awake, I'm wide awake, wide awake, I'm not sleeping"
- U2 – (Bad) *The Unforgettable Fire*

10850317R0

Made in the USA
Lexington, KY
24 August 2011